MORE PRAISE FOR LAWRENCE OSBORNE'S
THE BALLAD OF A SMALL PLAYER

"Hypnotic . . . Macau and Hong Kong feel vivid and true in the novel, yet also otherworldly: Well-known landmarks and weather conditions are captured with a stillness and beauty that make them feel haunting and melancholy. . . . But ultimately it is the uncertain fate of Doyle and the others that made me as a reader feel strangely fulfilled. The decisions they make seem connected to the thrilling and terrifying changes taking place around them. Old ways collide with a brash new world, and in this game it is not yet clear which will emerge the winner."

—Tash Aw, for *All Things Considered*

"Osborne masterfully recreates the atmosphere of casinos as well as the psychology of baccarat players—and leaves readers eager to try their luck at the game."

—*Kirkus Reviews*

"Osborne's *The Forgiven*, an *Economist* Best Book of the Year (and one of my personal bests from last year, too), is as brilliant, unsentimental a rendering of contemporary East-West conflict and the imperfect human psyche as you are likely to find. His new work proceeds in that tradition. . . . Don't miss."

—*Library Journal*

"[Osborne's] darkly introspective study of decline and decay conjures apt comparisons to Paul Bowles, Graham Greene, and V. S. Naipaul."

—*Booklist*

PRAISE FOR LAWRENCE OSBORNE'S
THE FORGIVEN

SELECTED BY THE *ECONOMIST* AS ONE OF THE
BEST BOOKS OF THE YEAR, 2012

SELECTED BY *LIBRARY JOURNAL* AS ONE OF THE
YEAR'S BEST BOOKS, 2012

YEAR'S BEST BOOKS CHOSEN BY WRITERS,
SELECTED BY LIONEL SHRIVER, THE *GUARDIAN*, 2012

"A sinister and streamlined entertainment in the tradition of Paul Bowles, Evelyn Waugh, and the early Ian McEwan . . . Surprising and dark and excellent."

—*New York Times*

"Extraordinarily acute to human nature."

—*Newsweek*

"A perfect storm of a novel."

—*Fredericksburg Free Lance-Star*

"A master of the high style."

—*Guardian*

"Osborne writes mercilessly, savagely well."

—*Daily Mail*

"Brooding, compelling . . . There's a strong, almost old-fashioned moral force at work in Osborne's novel. . . . At the novel's dramatic close, you could accuse Osborne of forcing the hand of moral come-uppance just a little too much—but it barely detracts from the tension he has maintained throughout the novel, and the pleasure of his bringing under such scrutiny the unpredictable behavior of his morally tortuous characters."

—*London Sunday Times*

"No mere imitation but a contribution to the shelf on which *The Sheltering Sky* and *The Bonfire of the Vanities* also sit . . . Osborne's writing is uncomfortably well observed; his story is sickeningly, addictively headlong."

—**Lionel Shriver, author of *We Need to Talk About Kevin***

The Wet and the Dry

The Forgiven

Bangkok Days

The Naked Tourist

The Accidental Connoisseur

American Normal

The Poisoned Embrace

Paris Dreambook

Ania Malina

THE

BALLAD

OF A

SMALL

PLAYER

LAWRENCE

OSBORNE

HOGARTH
LONDON / NEW YORK

Copyright © 2014 by Lawrence Osborne

Published in the United States by Hogarth, an imprint of the
Crown Publishing Group, a division of Random House LLC,
a Penguin Random House Company, New York.
www.crownpublishing.com

HOGARTH is a trademark of the Random House Group Limited,
and the H colophon is a trademark of Random House LLC.

Originally published in hardcover in the United States by
Hogarth, an imprint of the Crown Publishing Group,
a division of Random House LLC, New York, in 2014.

Library of Congress Cataloging-in-Publication Data
Osborne, Lawrence, 1958–
The ballad of a small player / Lawrence Osborne. — First edition.
pages cm
    1. British—China—Hong Kong—Fiction. 2. Gambling—China—
Hong Kong—Fiction. 3. Casinos—China—Hong Kong—Fiction.
I. Title.
PR6065.S23B36 2014
823'.914—dc23
2013035201

ISBN 978-0-8041-3799-7
eBook ISBN 978-0-8041-3798-0

Printed in the United States of America

Book design by Barbara Sturman
Cover design by Anna Kochman
Cover photography by Yiu Yu Hoi

10 9 8 7 6 5 4 3 2 1

First Paperback Edition

FAUSTUS:
*How comes it then that
thou art out of hell?*

MEPHISTOPHELES:
*Why this is hell,
nor am I out of it.*

—CHRISTOPHER
MARLOWE

THE

BALLAD

OF A

SMALL

PLAYER

At midnight on Mondays, or a little after, I arrive at the Greek Mythology in Taipa, where I play on those nights when I have nowhere else to go, when I am tired of Fernando's and the Clube Militar and the little brothel hotels on Republica. I like it there because there are no Chinese TV stars and because they know me by sight. It is one of the older casinos, archaic and run-down. Its woodwork reeks of smoke, and its carpets have a sweet rancid sponginess that my English shoes like. I go there every other weekend night or so, losing a thousand a week from my Inexhaustible Fund. I go there to scatter my yuan, my dollars, my *kwai*, and losing there is easier than winning, more gratifying. It's more like winning than winning itself, and everyone knows you are not a real player until you secretly prefer losing.

I like the bars stocked with Great Wall and Dragon Seal wine, which you can mix with Dr Pepper. I like the Greeks themselves. Zeus at the top of the gold staircase and the friezes of centaurs. I like the receptionists in cherry hats who sleep with you if you pay them enough. I even like the deserted traffic circle at the end of the street where I can go to catch my breath during a losing streak. The air in Macau is always sharp and clean, somehow, except when it's foul and humid. We are surrounded by stormy seas.

The crowd is mainlander at New Year: an outpouring of the nearby cities of Guangzhou and Shenzen and their choking suburbs. They look like crows, like swarms of birds. I wonder what they make of the murals of happy nymphs. Among them one can spot the safety-pin millionaires, the managers of the Pearl River factories, the mom-and-pop owners of manufacturing units specializing in computer keyboard buttons and toy cogs and gears for lawn mowers. All here to blow their hard-earned wads on the *I Ching*. The doors are of that bright gold that the Chinese love, the carpets that deep red that they also love and that is said to be the color of Luck. Droplet chandeliers plunge from ceilings painted with scenes from Tiepolo, with the zephyrs given Asian canthi. Corridor flowing into corridor, an endless system of corridors, like every Macau casino.

I pass into a vestibule. Red vases, where the glass screens are frosted with images of Confucius and naked girls. In a private room, briefly glimpsed, two Chinese players are laying down $100 HK bets every minute, but with a show of macho lethargy and indifference. One of them smokes an enormous cigar from the open box of complimentary Havanas on the table, flicking the ash into a metal conch shell intended to echo the cheap reproductions of Botticelli cut into the blue walls. My hands begin to sweat beneath the gloves I always wear inside the gaming houses. The smell that curls into my nose is that of humans concentrating on their bad luck, perspiring like me because of the broken fans.

The game here is punto banco baccarat. It involves no skill, and that is why the Chinese like it. Each table has a vertical electronic board upon which the patterns of Luck are displayed as mathematical trends in columns of numerals. The crowds gather around these boards to decide which tables are lucky and which are not. They scrutinize the lines of numbers, which change minutely with every hand that is played at the table. It is a way of computing the winds of change, the patterns of Luck, and I daresay the Western eye cannot read them at all. But then, they are not intended for our eyes.

I sit and take out my crocodile wallet. I play in yellow kid gloves and everyone there thinks I am a lord of some kind, a lord on the run with a unlucky streak that can be mitigated by the forces of the *I Ching*. The waiter asks me if I would like another drink, a bottle of champagne, perhaps? I order a bottle of something or other and

I think, *I'll drink it all anyway, sooner or later, I always do.* I never seem to get drunk either way. There is a middle-aged woman at the table and no one else. She looks over her spectacles toward me and there is the usual xenophobic hatred in her eye, and yet she is coquettish, she is a pro at the tables, she is dolled up in clothes from the malls in Tsim Sha Shui. She is playing with a mixture of mainland *kwai* and Hong Kong dollars, with a few tourist tokens thrown in. Easy pickings, she is thinking, looking at this plump *gwai lo* in his gloves and bow tie, with his look of a New England literature professor out on the town without permission from his wife. She looks me over, this bitch, and I enjoy the thought of skinning her alive with a few good hands. This encourages me to settle in.

The bets are $50 HK a hand. I begin to smoke, as I always do—Red Pagoda Hill and Zongnanha, the stuff that kills. The dealer gives me a little look. He, too, recognizes me; there are only a handful of *gwai lo* players in the whole city. "The wind," he says kindly, "is blowing the wrong way tonight." Bail out? *But,* I think, *the bitch is making money. She is sucking* my *money out of me.* No, no. "Keep at it," I say.

"Sure?"

"Sure."

I double my bets. I put down hundred-dollar bills on the three card plays and watch them disappear to the other side of the table. "One fifty," the woman says in Mandarin, tossing a green chip into the middle of an even greener table.

"Two hundred," I say in Cantonese.

"Two fifty."

"Three fifty!"

"All right," she sighs.

We play for four hands, and I lose three. A plate of bac-calau appears on the table and the woman picks up a plastic fork with undisguised relish. The *I Ching* is with her.

I now see how much gold she is wearing. I get up unsteadily and decide to backtrack to the men's room and cool off. The dealer hesitates and says, "Sir?" but I wave him down. "I'll be back," I say.

I never give up on the night until I am ready to fall down. I walk off, as if it doesn't matter to me at all. As if I really will come back from the men's room and skin her alive, and I am sure I will.

TWO

When I came back the older woman had disappeared. She had pulled her loot while ahead and was even now hauling a velvet bag of chips to the cashier. In her place another woman had sat down, but much more nervously and with a different weight to her hands. At a table, it is always the hands that I notice first. There are rapacious hands and expert ones, experienced hands and naïve ones, killer hands and victim hands. She was much younger, too. She perched at the far end of the table with a vulgar little handbag of the kind you can buy in the markets in Shenzen, badly made Fendi with gilt metal that flakes away after a week, and her left hand rested protectively on a small pile of lower-denomination red chips. She hoarded them in this way while her eyes scanned the surface of the table as if it were something she had never seen before. So she had sat at what she thought was an empty table. The bottle of champagne was still in its bucket, however. The waiter came up—he knew me—and said, in the heavy irony which the boys used with me in those days, "More champagne, Lord Doyle?"

As he said this, the girl's eyes rose for a moment. They shifted sideways to the electric number board behind me. The rows of yellow numbers had suddenly altered and I could hear them click, as if the luck force field were flicking them over like cards.

"Is that a change of luck?"

"It must be, your lordship."

We laughed. I was the jolliest loser. I turned in my seat and motioned to the girl.

"Why not ask the senhorita if she'd like a glass of champagne?"

He leaned down to my ear.

"Are you sure, sir?"

"Sure."

I pulled away from his whisper and gripped the neck of the bottle, extracting it from a rustle of ice.

"Why not?"

The waiter spoke to her in Mandarin. She said, "That's nice" in Cantonese. I spoke to her in the same language.

"It's vintage, you know, it's not just any old bubbly."

In the white noise of the sixty baccarat tables, where a crowd of munitions workers were hurling down their company-secured chips with curses and hoorahs, I thought for a moment that I had gone deaf, and when my hearing returned the girl was talking to me across a pall of smoke. She was saying *thank you* or some such thing, and her lips moved like two parallel fingers playing a game of rock-paper-scissors. They were overpainted, as was the style there. She wore a small crocus-white dress, and that was all I cared to notice. Not especially pretty, as the boy had been quick to observe. Not especially pretty but not especially unattractive either. She drank the champagne awkwardly, holding the glass with two fingers so that it almost fell, and I half wished I hadn't bothered.

We played for a while.

"Is it your first time?" I asked her between hands, as the machine shuffled the cards and the dealer twirled his pallet; her nod made him wonder as well.

"Over from Hong Kong for the night?"

"From Aberdeen."

"Aberdeen," I said. "I know Aberdeen."

Everyone does.

"I go there for Jumbo's."

"Ah," she said. "I go there on Sunday."

"There's a better place on Lamma," I went on. "Rainbow."

"Yes, I know it."

The Shuffle Master ejected three cards apiece. She handled them in the way that a buyer in a market will handle small fish before buying them. I wondered if she knew what she was doing, but one doesn't advise the enemy. She looked over the tops of the cards, and there was the crooked, up-country smile, the overapplied paints and creams. I won the next hand. It cheered me after a long hiatus, and the long ebbing of my chips was checked. I drank off the glass of Krug and ordered another bottle. There were two of us drinking now.

After two more winning hands I went to the cashier and bought more chips. The night was turning soft and bitter at the edges, and I wanted to be at the center of it for another hour. The boys winked at me because I was being picked up by a secretary, but even if I was I didn't particularly mind. Any man can be picked up by a woman half his age and he won't protest, he won't go kicking and screaming. He'll go along with it for a while, just to see what happens. I returned to my seat and as I brushed past the girl from Aberdeen I saw the gold chain resting around the back of her neck and the blue edge of a tattoo covered by her dress strap. The ink looked pretty against her olive skin. She looked up for a second as my gaze swept across her neck—a woman never lets this go—and she turned her cards against this same gaze, as if I might be cheating. The idea that I might made me smile. It would be like fleecing a lamb with a pair of nail scissors. I suppose it was because I had been coming there so long without talking to a fellow player that I felt inclined to be careful with her. I gradually detached myself from the hands I played, although I was winning again, and enjoyed the second bottle, which had been deposited in the ice bucket. The floor manager came by and wished me luck. His Sino-Portuguese eyes filled with cheerful malice and I said I was happy either way, winning or losing. The girl looked up. I could tell that she understood English well. She watched me pick up my cards, shift them, glance down at them without any outward sign of emotion, and I felt, for some reason, that we understood each other.

I walked out with her into the casino lobby, and there was the lilt in our walk, the agreement deep down at the level of the body.

"It's not my favorite place," I said grandly. "Have you been to the Venetian?" *I hate that, too,* my tone implied. She tried to smile back, but I could see that she was seesawing internally, weighing it up and down, this venture into a specific form of corruption. We walked out past the statue of Pegasus in the courtyard, and its wings were flapping, smoke blowing out of its nose, and the whores standing about in the parking lot were laughing at us.

I'm too old for you to worry about attraction, I wanted to say. *And I am sorry for that. It mortifies me, but I cannot change it.*

It was so crowded in this overblown courtyard that there was no room even to exchange a few words. She looked at her watch and said something about the hydrofoil back to Hong Kong, even though the last one didn't leave for a few hours, and in my experience with Chinese girls, when they are interested in you there is a very obvious slowing of their usual quickness of movement. She didn't slow. I let the comment melt away and then touched her hand for a moment and she turned to look at me and, in that flashing way, we had agreed upon it.

She spoke very quietly.

"Where can we go?"

"We can go anywhere. Not my room."

The light around us was a little brighter. Her bracelet was one of those multicolored childish objects from the Piper collection that are endorsed by Paris Hilton. She must have seen it in a magazine and let herself be persuaded into a mistake—the small circles of enamel didn't suit her at all. At least she wasn't wearing one of the hideous blue rings from the same maker. In the cab she would not touch me, aware perhaps of the prying eye of the Chinese cabbie fixed upon us in the rearview mirror (a *gwai lo* is always checked out), and I suggested an older, colonial place near the A-Ma temple where I had not been before and where—for some reason it mattered—I would not be recognized.

THREE

It rained along the shore. Along the embankments stand twisted fig trees planted by the Europeans, and they were still faintly visible in that darkness. Opposite, on the far side of the Van Nam Lake, rises a vision of China modern enough to chill the blood: the expressways, the towers, the garbled instruments of rising power. A terrible thing called the Cybernetic Fountain. But on the shore the old villas stand behind their sand-colored walls and the trees drip in the monsoon. There is a memory of ease, of the necessity of grace, white and lemon arches glimpsed between the fig trees. We passed near the temple as a soft thunder rolled in from the open sea. There are goddesses here who protect sailors and fishermen, and who protect the gambler, too.

The hotel lay at the top of a series of steep steps that wound around terrace garden patios with wizened trees and wet tables.

As I closed the door behind us, she said, "I am not the

usual prostitute. You think I am. But you may have made a mistake."

"Mistake?"

"I'm not a whore."

In the room we sat on the bed. There was the sound of the rain and the smell of flowerpots. I poured her a glass of wine from the mini-bar, but she didn't take it. Quite the contrary. There was no opening up. She held her legs closely together as her hands lay curled upward in her lap in an attitude of refusal, and perhaps, I thought, darkness was required. It was a venal thought, a crass thought. I went to the bathroom and turned on that light, then brought the bathroom door to within an inch of the jamb. That would be enough light for us, enough darkness to unlock her curious inhibitions. She brushed the water drops from her jacket and shivered. She asked for a towel to rub her hair. I took off my own jacket and then my shoes—it felt impudent, but there was nothing for it. She remarked on the rolling-off of the shoes and there was a disdain in her eyes, a sadness at the lack of imagination. Perhaps she really wasn't what I had thought.

She threw down the towel and decided to laugh her way out of this oncoming horror, because after all she could sense that I was not the usual customer. I wanted to apologize, and a woman can sense the imminence of a male apology. It's like a storm cloud on its way to hose you down.

I went to the table and laid a large *gift* next to her handbag, disposing of the question of money beforehand so that it would not ruin whatever moment we might share after the event.

In the humidity, the standard hotel flowers placed against the panes looked like things made out of a delicate rare stone. The corrugated leaves of geraniums as strange as small cabbages, the petals lying along the sills, and at around three the storm reached a crescendo. I let her sleep for a while.

On the night table her vanity bag sat with its clips opened, a hairbrush handle and some scented antiseptic hand wipes protruding. She snored lightly. Who was she? Dao-Ming Tang. An invented name, a circus name.

I wanted to leave, but there was no point running. And I could breathe in young skin, which is a nectar that becomes forbidden around the age of fifty-five. Gandhi sleeping between two young girls.

When she woke, she opened her eyes and they looked straight up at the lamp. She talked.

She said, "I thought you were very distinguished when I saw you sitting there with your yellow gloves. I've never seen anyone wear yellow gloves in a casino."

"They're my good-luck gloves."

"They're splendid. Only millionaires play in gloves."

"Is that right?"

She nodded.

We spoke in Cantonese, a slippery language for the white man, and she added, "They have those pearl buttons."

"Got them made in Bangkok."

"How classy."

"Not really. Classy would have been Vienna."

"Vienna?" she murmured.

Because it was just a word, and Vienna doesn't exist in the Chinese mind.

"I thought," she said, "you were a real gentleman. Like in the films."

She used the English word, *gentleman*.

"Gentleman?"

"Yes, a gentleman."

A gentleman, then.

"Maybe," she said very quietly, "you'll look after me."

"Is that what gentlemen do?"

"Yes."

She turned and laid her head against my shoulder.

"You're being modest. I know you are a lord."

There was nothing to say to this, and I let it go.

The prostitute and her client: the conversation of millennia. *Where are you from? What do you do?* The pleasure of lying. The woman, who is from a village in Sichuan called Sando, unknown to the masses. The lord, who is from a village in England where his father runs foxes and where the houses have pointed roofs, just as the films suggest. The lord and the whore.

"My village," she said, "has a temple with three stupas. I send money back every month to the monks so they can put gold on their deer. The temple has golden deer on its roof."

"You send money every month?"

She was quiet. I drank from the opened half bottle of wine, sitting on the edge of the bed while she watched me. I was glad that the darkness hid from her the quiet ruin of my body, and that because of the rain we did not have to talk much.

"You must have a lot of money," she said later on. "To stay in a place like this. All the other men run out of money."

"I win and I lose, like everyone else."

"Lord Doyle," she laughed.

"It sounds silly, doesn't it?"

"No," she said. "It just sounds funny. Not silly. I'm sure you win more than you lose."

"I practice every day."

"I saw how you play."

"How is that?"

"Like a gentleman. Like you don't care. Like tossing something to the wind."

"Oh?"

"Yes. Careless like a lord."

She smiled behind her hand.

"It's not what you think," I protested. "I'm not what you think."

"I know," she countered. "I'm not as silly as you think I am."

Who could say where her curiosity about me came from? It was an instant mystery whipped up out of nowhere. You might even call it an instant liking, a sympathy that had blown up in a matter of seconds like the affinity that blossoms between children in the space of a single minute.

"That's how I am," I admitted a bit self-importantly. "I want to lose it all. It's idiotic, I know. I should be embarrassed."

"Then you're a real gambler."

I finished the bottle and rolled it under the bed.

"That's me. I've always been like this."

"Not me," she said. "I hate gambling. I hate gamblers."

Yes, I thought, *you probably do.*

"I hate it when they win," she added.

And I wondered if I hated myself when I won. It was possible.

"Well, I am a loser," I said. "You should like me a bit more."

"Shall we sleep?" she said sweetly.

She lay and folded her hands together under her chin, and I thought there was something pleased and secure in the way she closed her eyes and let herself drift off without any fuss.

My mind filled with mathematical images and scores as I dozed against her and the sex was expended. The cards flipped by a cheap spatula, a thousand plays streaming through the dark and my eye calculating them all. A man who cannot love, but who can scan the statistics of the laws of chance. It was too late to regret how I had turned out.

But all the same I felt differently this time, and in small, aggravating ways. I couldn't say why it was. Something about her had made me feel ashamed and I felt myself spinning out of my orbit, wondering to myself whose daughter she was and where she had come from, questions that never troubled me usually. I felt ponderous and accused, and something in me retreated and tried to hide. For the first time I wondered to myself what I looked and felt like to a woman of her age, a woman in her late twenties, I imagined; how repulsive I must be, how oppressive and pitiful. I knew those things before, of course. One is never that self-deluding. It's the other way around: a man knows everything inferior about himself, but there's nothing to be done. He grits the teeth and gets through it. I picked up one of these girls once a month, and it was like a duty, a visit to the confessional. There was nothing else in Macau. The gambler who lives here is not going to find a normal wife. It's a life sentence for some and I had lived like this for years, stumbling from one encounter to the next and never caring because I knew I had nothing better to look forward to. But now, suddenly, the known system had stopped working and I was forced to look at the invisible mirror, and the shocking image there made me want to be blind. It was the way she slept against me, trustingly, and never showed her disgust, which must have been so deep that it could not express itself. I was not used to that.

I could never have told her my real reasons for being there, my long, rather comical flight from the law after a certain *unpleasant incident* in England long ago. One learns not to reveal a single thing to anyone, not even to a woman who is sharing one's bed for a while, and after a time this secrecy becomes second nature, an unchallenged mode of behavior. There cannot be any slip-ups. One doesn't fancy being shipped back to Wormwood Scrubs to serve one's time. Not at all. One wants to be free in the world of money, or even chained inside it so long as its marvels are available.

I half-slept curled against that sad little back, and I could smell the talc on her shoulders and the after-scent of pork buns. I dreamed of the river Ouse and the church in Piddinghoe. Thunder from out at sea rolled in and shook the placid little garden outside the window, and I tightened my grip around her and wondered if she would remember me this time the following night, or any of the following nights, or whether she would even remember the room itself when she was old. It would all be lost. When

I woke up the shutters were still closed and a cat had appeared on the outside sill, nosing the gap between them. For a moment I thought I was in England and my fingers gripped the edge of the bed in a panic. Then I remembered everything about China, which was now my home. Dao-Ming was gone, as they always are. The sheet had not gone cold, however, and slightly oiled hairs stuck to the pillowcase that, when picked out, fell limp across my fingers like things that had just died. They smelled of patchouli and storms, and I thought how serious and stilted our chats had been and how unlike the usual chats I have with my purchased roses.

The rain continued as if nothing had happened, and deep within myself I was sure that I would see her again, because although the city is a reef where the confused fish never meet twice unless a goddess intervenes, intervene she sometimes does. Solitude and loss are the rule, and years go by before one realizes it, but one can always meet a woman twice in a city. It's not like living on the mainland, lost among the billions. There are hundreds of Dao-Mings, and thousands of Tangs, but a connection made is a connection never forgotten, or almost not forgotten, and one day, I was sure, I would once again find the girl who generously gilded the deer of Sando.

FOUR

The following night at eight exactly, I put on my darkest suit and took the elevator down from the seventh floor of the Hotel Lisboa. It was the hour of the "second shift" in the world's most profitable casino, and the revolving doors turned like turbines as crowds poured through them and hurled themselves toward the labyrinth of casinos scattered throughout the hotel. Seven million dollars a day in revenues and a pall of smoke that never moved, that hovered near the tops of the tangerine trees from which hung a thousand red New Year envelopes like venomous fruit. Smoke that hit the throat like sawdust mixed with powdered metal.

I went down to the hotel's main mass-market casino, the Mona Lisa, where the games are endless in their diversity: *pai kao, fanton, cussec, Q*, and stud poker, and of course punto banco baccarat, that slutty dirty queen of casino card games. The boys brought me a cognac and sausage rolls, and I ordered a buttonhole from the street.

Cut a figure, O my brothers, and have them believe that you really are a lord. But I lost again. I played fish-prawn-crab dice for an hour, forgetting myself completely, then moved off down the elevators to the Crystal Palace, which is like descending into an ice grotto. Waves of glass shards fall from the ceilings in shades of green and orange. A place where the rational mind comes apart. From there I navigated in total solitude to the Club Triumph and the Lisboa Hou Kat, a place that has a secretive feel to it, like a buried palace in Crete from the time of Linear B, with a circular room of leather sofas and tangerine trees with New Year envelopes. How can such places exist?

The hours passed. The money slipped away. A bead of sweat at the base of the spine, and my sweet vertigo. After a long losing spree I went back to my room to freshen up, then took the elevator down to the casinos for a second try. It was eleven and the night shift was just in. Brutal, cynical men with red faces and cheap suits, smoking continuously, their eyes little lusty slits that sucked everything in and spat it out again. On the ground floor they stood by the Throne of Pharaoh, a reproduction chair from Tutankhamen's tomb, and a large vertical oil painting with its title provided: *La Mère Abandonnée.* A woman with a lyre sighing over a baby sleeping in a wheeled carriage. This scene of rural misery from nineteenth-century France did not arouse their curiosity at all, and they turned their backs to it as they waited for the elevators. They carried bags of gaming chips and cans of winter melon tea. Their breath smelled of oyster sauce. I bought a cigar in the underground mall and went back up to the VIP rooms, where Renoirs loomed on the walls. Here in the four innermost rooms the bets were a minimum of ten thousand up to a maximum of two million. Three plays at a time, usually. There was a separate entrance leading into the hotel to encourage the high rollers to roll right out of bed and into the VIP rooms with sleep in their eyes. Bright red armchairs had dropped out of the surrounding Alma-Tadema paintings of ancient Rome. Laughing maidens gamboling down flowery slopes. Air and light and lust. Scenes from the second century, or the first century, or the fourth century, or the never-never century. So many centuries reduced to a mural. So many centuries of pointless pleasure. And here the factory managers who had never read a book about Rome, much less visited, sat and lounged and tensed their minds as they threw themselves like disoriented moths against Luck's candle flame. They didn't know where they were. Eastwest.

I played side baccarat for a while, and I was impressed by the way the staff brought me my supply of chips, like men stoking an engine fire in a train. I cheered up as my luck improved; I won three hands out of six. Four hundred back in. The myth paintings grew pinker as the hours went by. I became jolly again and won two hands more. I felt a stab of sadistic vitality.

With a modest profit I retired to the armchairs, in the décor of Paris 1900, and marveled at the gold mosaic floors of the elevators, which shone for a moment as the doors opened. I had made about $600 HK—it was nothing to brag about, but it wasn't a loss. Peanuts add up.

An hour later I migrated back to the Crystal Palace, where the air was sweet and heavy with female perfumes. Teenage girls aplenty. Hong Kong men in blue suits. I lost it all and then some. It's the way it goes, and I didn't care. It was well after midnight by the time I got down to the new Sands and strode through that monumental hall whose din makes you feel mad and happy at the same time—not *exactly* the same time, but close.

I was feeling more reckless than I usually do, and the losses that I sustained on the slot machines did not serve to deter me from getting into deeper water. When did losses ever do that? I went to the first-floor buffet restaurant and sat there calculating my losses and my remaining reserves. The math was simple, but sliding. The fact was that after several months of playing the tables almost nonstop every night I had burned through the greater part of the money I had saved up over the years and had brought to Macau. A small fortune that had been supposed to last me a fair while, assuming that on average I would win almost as much as I lost, or maybe even more. But it had not worked out that way. It never does.

After a glass of Lello Douro, I made my way past the floor show and the Jade Monkey slot machines to the entrances of the separate private gaming rooms. I was guided by staff dressed in the yellow uniforms of the witch's guards in *The Wizard of Oz*, who took me right to the door, assuming, I suppose, that I was a high roller. I was certainly tempted by the nearby roulette tables, with names like Lucky Seals and Fairy's Fortune, but since I was now resolved upon risking a much bigger sum of money, I let myself be escorted upstairs to the Paiza Club, at that time the most exclusive private gaming room in Macau. Besides, everyone knows that roulette lends a 2.7 advantage to the house, no matter what you do. For baccarat it's a mere 0.9.

The staff upstairs were in black and gold uniforms with gold buttons. I was surprised to hear that they already knew my name.

"Lord Doyle," they said, swinging a welcoming hand toward the rooms called pits, which were arranged around a circular structure only half revealed by a luxurious dimness.

The atrium was cavernous, with a huge tasseled lantern suspended at its center. The style was very Chinese.

Terra-cottas in niches and dragons everywhere. The world's biggest chandelier, my escort said, indicating it with her hand. I was then given a choice of private rooms, some of them with fires in grates, bloodred panels, and gray tables. I chose a room where I could play against the bank alone with $10,000 HK hands.

I sat myself down there and waited for a bottle of wine to be brought up from the cellar. I took off my gloves and the banker bowed to me and announced his name, which was unusual. We relaxed into some anticipatory banter and then I was given my chips.

It was by now nearing dawn and the other rooms had their occupants, wealthy punters from the Territories in sleek suits, with briefcases of money laid at their feet like waiting dogs.

I settled down with a cigar courtesy of management and played a few hands at a more relaxed pace than I am used to. I had to admit to myself that the game was much more enjoyable played like this, without the hustle and bustle of a Chinese mob around me, at my own pace and without the internal tension that usually drove me forward. I thought a little more carefully about what I was doing. These are the ideal conditions for gaming if the individual doesn't want to lose a lot of money quickly on a series of small, fast bets. The game is the same, but the ambience is not.

It was now that I felt the compulsion that always

drives me from within as I see the pallet turn the cards and I feel them slipping like skin under my finger pads. A sensual moment, empty but charged with anticipation. The mind emptying out like a drain, or else scurrying like a small, wingless bug.

There are a few moments of this total calm before I start to move, like the moments that I imagine precede jumping off a cliff. Even in these exclusive rooms the dealer will tell you the table's "luck numbers" if you ask him, and there will be a place in your mind that wrestles with the superstition.

The gambler is a man finely tuned to the supernatural. He is superstitious, wary of portents and omens. He is on edge for this reason. I wear kid gloves at the table, a habit in which I had indulged those past two years, and this was also a superstition. I put them on at the last moment after I have felt the cards, and through their supple material I feel the laminated surfaces all over again. I feel ready to win or lose.

Lose, in this case. It didn't matter so much this time because I had written off any losses that night in advance. I did not sweat it as the first ten grand hit the dust. I poured myself another glass of wine. The dealer rolled back on his heels and asked me if I felt confident enough to go up to fifteen thousand, and perhaps provoked by the undertow of his tone, I said that I would.

"Good for you, sir. Courage often wins."

Does it? I thought. *Does it really play a part in out-comes?*

"It's a superstition," I replied.

A manager came in then and shook my hand. He was beautifully dressed and he asked me if everything was to my satisfaction.

"Lord Doyle, isn't it?"

"Well, if you say so."

He laughed.

"I do say so."

The dealer then bowed.

"Do you like the cards? Special from Germany," the manager said. "Binokel with Württemberg artwork."

I glanced down; they were indeed unusual.

"They are fine."

"Mr. Hui here will look after you. He is one of our best bankers. We can bring you some light dishes if you need them. Do you?"

"I'm not hungry."

"As you prefer."

I felt the sweat now moving slowly down my back, clinging to the spine, an area of moistness developing between my eyes. When the manager had retired, I asked Mr. Hui if I might have some iced water with some lemon juice. While waiting for it, I looked over the English eques-trian paintings on the walls and the iron dogs of the fire-place. It reminded me of an actual room I had seen in

England, a room in a large country house that I had been in once upon a time, perhaps a famous country house. I tried to think if I knew those long, aquiline faces of long-dead noblemen, their Caucasian faces subtly distorted by copiers not familiar with them. One of them might have been the real Lord Doyle for all I knew. I wondered if indeed there was one, or whether I had chosen my Macau name with inspired good luck all those years ago. I half-remembered, in fact, reading the name in a newspaper somewhere and it must have stuck in my unconscious. Alternatively, perhaps, I had been to a house where Lord Doyle was mentioned or represented. I could no longer remember.

Yet the past, at that particular moment, was suddenly vividly present. I became distracted and lost my focus. Memories that I had long repressed must have been aroused in me by the cold sweat running in a trickle down my back, but why would a trickle of sweat make me think of my long-lost days in Cuckfield, I wondered. Though then again perhaps I had heard of a Lord Doyle in that Sussex village where I had lived for years as a lawyer, and it was possible he might even have been one of our firm's clients. It was unlikely, however. I looked again at the Binokel cards and I felt myself lost in time, and I was sure that it must have been because of this intensely English and nostalgic décor in which I was now immersed. The cartoon lords were staring down at me as if I owed them money. No one in China knew why I was there, why I was sitting there at that very moment looking down at some Binokel cards after almost a decade in exile. They never asked why I never went home, or even if I had a home. They were never indiscreet enough to ask, and even if they had asked I would not have been able to tell them. It was not a pretty story I could recount over dinner.

I had been accused of an embezzlement with regard to one of my elderly clients, and I had not departed in a way that reflected well upon me. It had been a flight under cover of dark, a sudden *sauve qui peut*. I had not even told my sisters. The money was gone from the lady's account and it was I who was in charge of that account, and worse than that I had spent everything and could not restore it. The directors of the firm had discovered the matter on a Thursday; by Friday night I was out of the country with a suitcase of money that I took with me and did not declare. The bulk of the money had already been wired to Hong Kong.

The lady I had stolen it from was one of those elderly widows one sees everywhere holed up secretively in the suburban houses of Haywards Heath or Wivelsfield, in the timbered Tudor mansions of Hassocks or Cuckfield or Lindfield. Plump townlets and manicured villages filled with colonial and military retirees and outpastured bank managers, with their yew hedges and their grumbling lawns and their churches filled with tattered flags. This was the world into which I was born, having won (as Cecil Rhodes once had it) first draw in the lottery of life: born an Englishman.

Mrs. Butterworth was married to a copper mining executive and had inherited all his money. They had once lived in South America, and her house retained a strange and faint tropicality. She loved caged birds and dark yellow silks, and there was a sunroom at the back of the house that seemed to rise to the occasion even of a dull English summer. The husband had been dead a quarter century. It's possible that I reminded her of him. A young man in a dark suit, with hesitant manners. But I must have been more insecure than her former husband. He had gone to Rugby and belonged to a decent London club—I think it was even White's. It is possible that she was too senile already to notice these unfortunate aspects of her well-groomed visitor. Perhaps she didn't care to look too closely. I was able to fake the accent and the easy charm, and it is likely that she took these at surface value and didn't look further.

We were soon having tea together every week. She was obsessed with her savings and her investments, and being a creature of intuition and habit she refused to discuss these with anyone else at the firm. Every Thursday morning I walked from the firm's offices to her timbered mock-Tudor on Summerhill Lane and pulled the iron bell chain set into the door and waited under a fringe of honeysuckle for her padded step. We took Earl Grey and sandwiches in the sunroom, and she talked about her husband. She called him "my glorious Teddy."

"Oh, my glorious Teddy organized everything for me before he died," she would say, forgetting that she had said the very same thing the week before. "But now I seem to have got into a tizzy about it all. He always told me to move my money around and keep it fresh. Do you agree?"

"Your husband was perfectly correct."

"But there's no one I trust, you see." Her eyes shone with a kind of crazy flinty gullibility. "Except you, of course. Perhaps you could take some of my funds out of Rio Tinto and put them somewhere else? I am going to authorize Mr. Ashburton at Lloyd's to give you access. Now, why don't you try one of my chutney sandwiches? I make the chutney myself with Mr. Porter's raisins from Sunte Avenue. Go on."

She barely recognized me in the later days, when I came by to chat with her and hold her hand and assess the value of her moldering but well-stocked property. She sometimes thought I was her nephew, or the doctor, or who knows who else. While she dozed in her armchair in the front room, I wandered through her mansion and pocketed, for fun, the occasional trinket. She never noticed. And so I began to steal from her very gradually, a hundred pounds here, a hundred pounds there, and when

I progressed to higher sums I saw that it made no difference. No one was watching over her affairs but me, and no one had access to her bank account but me. There must have come a point, I reflected as I sat there looking at the Binokel card, when I realized that I could get away if not with murder then with the second best thing.

I must have passed the better part of two years laboring at this secret game. I became, gradually, much richer than anyone around me, and much richer than I myself had ever been before—because I had never been even well off, let alone seriously affluent. Quite the contrary. I came from the loins of a vacuum cleaner salesman. I had never had anything. In fact I had noticed, hitherto, a certain snobbery toward me on the part of the other lawyers at our firm, and certainly a distinct snobbery coming from the partners. They could tell by a sixth sense that I was not one of them. I had not gone to a public school, not even Ardingly, down the road, where most of them had spent their miserable boyhoods loafing around willowed ponds. I had been to the local state schools. To Scrayes Bridge Comprehensive and then Haywards Heath Grammar, where I had picked up my A levels. I was an orphan in the Hindu-style English caste system, a "ghost" indeed. To them I was therefore faintly detestable, comically inferior, and they were a little surprised, I imagine, that I had even made it that far. Nottingham was not a bad university but it didn't exactly ring any bells; it had no meaning to the boys who had come down from Oxford and King's. The only thing that confused them was my accent.

As I say, I had studied their accent and reproduced it. As the country as a whole went more and more prole in its accents, I went the other way and I did it on purpose, because of course now I was at war with it all and I wanted to win at parody while siphoning off as much of Mrs. Butterworth's money as I could. I stashed it away in various accounts and soon I had an account in Hong Kong, which I was able to open with the help of a friend. It proved to be invaluable. Into Hong Kong I poured all my secrets and hopes. It seemed then like the land of freedom and invisibility.

China. A police state would not seem the ideal place for escape. But what if it was a police state that didn't like our police? My enemy's enemy is my friend. No one would go looking for me in a place like Macau, because Macau wasn't Hong Kong; it was one of the most secretive places on earth. I thought about it a great deal as I paced around Haywards Heath at night, that empty and tomblike place in which only the railway line is a source of life after midnight. It could not be any worse, I thought, than the prison I was already living in. Lodging in a private flat with Mrs. Eaglin on Denman's Lane, riding to work on a bicycle when it wasn't raining. A company car, otherwise, a Vauxhall Astra perfect for country lanes but terminally undistinguished. The only thing that redeemed this unworthy existence was the idea that I could get away with the Butterworth dosh. It was a strange thought that I was acquiring all the wealth of that long-dead mining executive. Anglo-American Copper and its tributaries, a vile company in all likelihood, and its treasures had ended up in my secret bank account in Hong Kong. Why would it be immoral to gamble that money away? Would that be worse than the way it had been gained? I remembered how guiltless I had felt, the first time I spent a week in Hong Kong on holiday. Within days I knew the Macau casinos back to front.

It seemed to me that unlike the snobbish and closed world from which I came, this place had a violent democracy about it. I compared it to Haywards Heath and I was charmed. I formed the idea of eloping there with my spoils. A foolish idea, no doubt, childish and naïve. But I was sure that sooner or later the directors would smoke me out, as indeed they eventually did. I didn't want to go back to the unworthy existence, let alone face psychiatric evaluation and possibly prison, and wanted to keep Mrs. Butterworth's money, which otherwise would have been sent to the International Society for the Humane Treatment of Marine Mammals.

It was a tense wire to be balanced upon, and I was a poor tightrope walker. One afternoon the senior partner of our firm, Mr. Strick, invited me into his office at the top of the building and frostily asked me to take a seat. He was a very old-school character, much like Mr. Butterworth, I imagine, and he believed in the sterling value of "man-to-man" chats.

"Look here, Doyle," he said, taking off his glasses and inserting one of the grips into the corner of his mouth, "I've always thought you were a rather decent chap, even if you do keep yourself to yourself a bit too much. Some of the others were wondering if a chap like you might feel a tad uncomfortable with chaps like them. I said, he's a funny old chap and that's all there is to it. What do you say, Doyle? No after-work pints for you?"

"I'm not much of a drinker, sir."

"Ah, so that's it, eh, you're not a chap who likes to drink too much?"

"No, sir."

How could I forget that office, with its paperweights filled with pieces of Pacific coral and the golf clubs in glass cases? That smell of shag and woodland mud and stale PG Tips?

"Well, look here, old chap, I've noticed that you've been eating every lunch at Tiffany's French place across the roundabout. Rather dear for you, isn't it?"

"I've developed a taste for it, sir."

"Yes, yes. But what I mean is, Doyle, you seem to have a bit of money to knock around. I'm not aware we gave you a raise."

We laughed, and for the first time I had an inkling of

his suspicion, of the close eye that he was keeping on me. "Everything all right with the Butterworth account? You and Mrs. Butterworth seem awfully tight. You are going there every week? It must be a frightful bore."

"Not at all. We talk about old films."

"Do you now? She seems like a frisky old bird. I knew her husband, you know. We played golf together at Ardingly. Spiffing chap and all that, but a bit morose for my taste. They say he made a lot of money in precious metals. But I suppose you'd know all about that."

I said that I did, and that I took great interest in the account.

"Good show," he concluded, putting his glasses back on. "But, Doyle—we do have to keep an eye on Mrs. Butterworth. She is not quite in her right mind. I wouldn't want any irregularities to occur."

At that moment, in Macau, I looked up from the elaborately designed cards and into the eyes of the English seigneurs on their thoroughbreds. I hated nothing more than them. I saw the puffed face of Mrs. Butterworth laid back against an antimacassar. She had been sweet and arrogant in equal measure. A woman who looked down on me when she had had her wits about her. I had taken her hand when I entered the room and spoken to her close to, stooped to the ear. *Yes, Mrs. Butterworth; no, Mrs. Butterworth.*

"Are you the lawyer chap?" she had asked over and again. "My husband says never trust a lawyer. He says you're all cheerful scum."

When I returned to business I was revived by the cold water. I played two hands of fifteen each, losing one and winning one. I was emboldened to ratchet it up to twenty, at which point I had to unseal the second of the padded envelopes of cash I had brought with me.

I laid the money out and got my cards. I was sure, in that moment, that someone was watching me from behind one of the paintings (I assumed they had observation windows built into them) and when I turned my hand to reveal a four and a six, I was sure that someone somewhere had smiled. A four and a six is a baccarat, a zero hand worth nothing, or to be technical, a ten modulo ten: the worst hand you can draw. It was as crushing a losing hand as I could have pulled, and the dealer himself shook his head empathetically before awarding me a commiseration of sorts. He wished me better fortune for the next play.

"I drew a baccarat yesterday," I said. "Two in two days."

"Tut tut."

"I am not smelling the winds."

I paused and dabbed my forehead with a cocktail napkin, because a moment before everything had seemed so clear—even if only for a few seconds—and now I no longer knew if I should play another hand or go home with half my envelope intact.

"You want a pause, sir?"

"I can't lose twice with a baccarat."

As the table was prepared, the sound of the *erhar* rose up from somewhere, and I thought it must be dawn outside, or close. I waited for my mind to calm and clear and then laid my twenty thousand on the table.

"Are you sure this time?" the dealer asked politely.

I flipped the first card and noted the five. The dealer looked at me suavely, and I think he was genuinely curious. The coal fire crackled behind us, and his back must have been warm. I turned a four and won the hand with a natural. Surprised, he stepped back for a moment. He raised a moist hand towel to his mouth and nodded a mute congratulation. I sat back and watched the chips pushed my way, a great salacious pile of them, and I paused to smoke for a few minutes. I may have imagined it, but I thought I heard a bell ringing somewhere deep inside the complex of pits. What kind of bell, I had no idea. Perhaps a bell went off whenever a punter made a large winning.

The dealer shuffled the cards again and we took our ease, bantering about the trade. He then asked me if I felt inclined to take on another hand. I was now feeling roused, aggressive. A sudden win will do that to you. It will lift you out of months of depression and self-doubt, days of quiet dread. A surge of animal arrogance of the kind that one needs to feel in order to remember that you are alive. Doomed to be alive.

"Lady Luck is with me," I said in English.

He dealt my two cards and I turned a three and a two. He therefore dealt me a third card. It was a four.

"Natural," he said, raising his eyebrows for a moment and then stepping back from the table with a slight twitch of the head.

I looked at my watch and saw that it was five thirty-five a.m. I could feel the wind of fortune switching direction around me like something physical, a real breeze admitted by a door suddenly opened. I stood and bagged the mound of chips as the manager came in a second time and congratulated me, bowing and hoping that I would return to the Paiza soon.

"We welcome you anytime, Lord Doyle."

I was given a small attaché case for the cash and escorted politely to the main doors, where a tour bus from Shenzen had just arrived, offloading fresh crowds for the main floors of the Sands. I went through to get to the main road, shrugging off their overdoses of scent, and soon I was walking into Avenida da Amizade. I didn't even know exactly how much it was: hundreds and hundreds of thousands. Kenny Rogers had it right. You never count your money when you're sittin' at the table.

I walked back to the Lisboa in the dawn, past the yawning molls of the Rua de Pequim and the Fortuna casino, passing by that strange fragment of the Rue de Rivoli. Inside the Lisboa lobby I gave my case to reception so that they could entrust it to the house safe, and then I wandered around the galleries, staring at those antique ink stones and Chinese seismographs that seem to be permanently on sale there. There was a jade galleon, too, and farther down a gilded peacock from Garrard's of London displayed with a glass of blue wine next to it. The luxury goods that I passed every day without much noticing them. And finally I came to a spinach-green jade figure of Guan Yin herself standing next to a pendulum clock of the same material.

Properly, it is Guashi'yin. They shorten it to Guan Yin. She is a bodhisattva. Her name means *listening to the sounds of the world.* Or, one could put it, listening to the *cries* of the world. Because she is also the goddess of mercy and compassion. For the Taoists she is an immortal. She is the female form, in East Asia, of the Indian male bodhisattva Avalokiteshvara.

I stood there for some time, mentally lost inside that lustrous greenness, the face and eloquent hands of a jade bodhisattva, and something within me began to revolve, to change direction, and I felt how impossible it would be to just go upstairs and go to sleep. My victory had crystallized and now it fragmented again like a glass ball dropped from a great height. I turned and walked calmly back to reception.

"Give me the case back," I said. "Yes, all of it."

Their looks were questioning, but after all they didn't care.

I walked back to the Paiza, where the doormen greeted me without surprise. Over the next hour I proceeded to lose most of what I had with me, but thereafter my fortune revived a little and I swung between light and dark, between surplus and deficit. It was almost midday before I got to bed. I had left neither worse off nor better, and the next night (for there was always a next night; my life was a series of next nights) I went down more confidently in my smoking jacket with the velvet lapels and sat at the larger fourteen-person baccarat tables between nine and ten.

Perhaps it was the sleep. I was now loaded with betting power, though of the negative kind, and I was feeling belligerent, aggressive, so unsure of myself that I was sure of myself. I was the only *gwai lo* there that night, and the regulars who knew me glanced at me with their usual contempt.

No matter. I had their measure, the little scum. If I lost again I'd do it with an exceptional indifference that would show them who was who in the pecking order of life. I took the case with me and when I opened it to pull out an enormous sum to place my first bet, the other players paled and bit their lips. These were small-timers, or medium-timers, and they weren't used to heavy bets. I was discreetly advised to perhaps split my bets into smaller sums. As a matter of fact I was happy to oblige. I didn't need to win on one big killing. I split my treasure into $500 HK shots and played them one by one, eleven in a row. Complete success.

I looked up at the numbers board and saw new digits slip into place, changing its complexion. My table was now announced as highly fortunate. A slightly larger crowd developed around it. Onlookers pressed in, smoking with wild intensity until the table was thickly shrouded with smoke. I heard their guttural oaths and expressions of disbelief in their crude Putonghua, their imprecations against the dirty foreigner and his goddamned luck. I could understand every word and they didn't know it, but I let it go. I won and won. Chips rolled in, waves of them.

At ten thirty I got up and bagged the lot, taking them over to the cashier's window followed by dozens of stares. I bundled the cash into my attaché case and rolled out of there, moving on to the Hong Fak, certain that I had scored at least a half million, which I probably had. It was a decent day's work.

FIVE

The prince of card games was introduced into France from Italy during the reign of Charles VIII and is similar in some ways to systems like faro and basset. It is the simplest of the card games and also the most honest from the point of view of the punter. It's hard for the house to cheat at baccarat, and there is a satisfying instant gratification to its simplicity and relative speed. It kills you quickly.

There are three variations played in different parts of the world: chemin-de-fer, banque, and the North American version, punto banco. This last is the kind played in China and it is a pure game of chance, with no skill involved. The player's moves are forced by the cards, whereas in the two other versions the player can make choices, which allows skill to play a part in the outcomes. The rules are as follows.

The game is played with eight decks of cards, which are dealt by three bankers. Each player is given two cards, traditionally by a *shoe* that moves up and down the table. It couldn't be more simple. Whoever turns the highest-scoring hand wins the round. Cards two to nine are worth face value, tens and face cards—jack, queen, or king—are worth nothing, and an ace is valued at one. Players calculate their hands by adding up the values, then subtracting the ten digit if that total is higher than ten. This is known as modulo ten.

For example, a hand of six and eight is worth four: six plus eight equals fourteen modulo ten. If the hand is a four and five, however, then it stands at nine. And nine is the highest value a baccarat hand can be. It is called a *natural* and conquers all other hands.

There are three options for betting: the banker (banco), the player (punto), and what is known as *tie*. These do not necessarily correspond to the actual banker or player; they are merely betting options. The cards are dealt facedown, first to the player and then to the banker, and are turned by the banker. He establishes what is called the *tableau*, the state of play. If a natural is turned, then the game is over and the lucky holder of the perfect nine is the winner. If not, a player has the right to a third card if he has drawn five or less.

It is usual for the player to be paid even money while the banker collects ninety-five percent, with five percent to the house. Some casinos pay even money to both player and banker except where the banker wins by a six; he is then paid fifty percent of the bet. If the player and banker hands are equal, then a tie is called and both are paid at odds of eight to one.

It's difficult to explain what makes baccarat so compelling. Because it is such a high-stakes game, sometimes played at ten thousand dollars a hand, gaming corporations may see their entire quarterly profits or losses affected by a single night's play. You can win or lose millions in a short space of time, and so can the house. It has danger, a steel edge to it; it is a game of ecstasy and doom. There is nothing like it in the gambling universe. It was the game of kings and nobles, a game of tycoons, and now it is the game of the Chinese masses. But it is still the game of the reckless rich.

Punto banco baccarat is a struggle with the pure laws of chance. When you play it you are alone with your fate, and one is not often alone with one's fate. When you play it your heart is in your mouth. Your pulse quickens to an unbearable pace. You feel that you are walking along the edge of the volcanic precipice made of sharp, hot rock cut as fine as a razor and capable of breaking with all the drama of glass. It is a game surrounded by threatening possibilities: instant death, which comes even quicker than it does with poker or roulette. That's what I like about it. There's no lingering illusion. Death by guillotine.

•   •   •

I spent that day in bed with the curtains drawn. Nothing kept me conscious, not even the rain pounding against the windows or the construction crews below. I dreamed without noise or commotion or imagery, but with a dread that was like being tied up on a chair and sensing the approach of someone behind you armed with a meat cleaver. Ants massing on a tiled floor, the flap of linen curtains at a window somewhere in the tropics. At one point it was just raging sea. I was dreaming of a raging sea and the rage was in slow motion, extended to hours of repetitive wave formations.

Then I woke, and it was night. The sky was lit with neon and signs for massage girls. SUZIE, BABYLON GIRLS, MEGA. One read YUMMY. My wrists, the sides of my throat were damp. I took a hot bath. I then lay there trying to empty my mind completely as it prepared for a long night of noisy solitude and concentration. A night of combat with Lady Luck, a night of seesaws. I had no plan of action other than to trust for a second night in the I Ching, which was working its effects through my unconscious. I must have cottoned on to something unconsciously, I thought, without any rational effort, and all I had to do was continue as I was doing and it might turn out all right. The less I thought, the better. Always the best plan, nonthought. And it was paradoxical, but I was sure I would win if I continued just trusting in my own unconscious. The unconscious is merely misunderstood. It's not a trickster.

I dressed up that night. Tuxedo and tie. New laces, and a dab of Romeo. One has to be reckless sometimes, to spend what one doesn't have. I went down to Galera, the Robuchon restaurant on the third floor.

The elevator opens directly into its atrium, in which a glass display of old wine stands, rows of Petrus '61 and Cheval Blanc '66, Sauternes from the fifties and the odd bottle of La Tâche. The Lisboa's owner, Stanley Ho, is China's greatest wine connoisseur and he can stock his Robuchon outlet with whatever wines he wants. It's the food and wine temple of Macau, the millionaire's crux.

I asked if I could put everything on my account.

"If you insist, sir."

"I do insist."

I sat by the windows. The smell of pricy tarts rose high, tarts like chocolate boxes, but unwrapped and opened up to the consumer. I ordered a bottle of Kweichow Moutai from 1927, a liquor made from sorghum that people say is the most expensive Chinese beverage ever made. It was $47,500 HK on the list: perfumed, slightly desiccated. I drank it with some yellow and green crab cakes, then avocado and mango mixed in with the crab. I knew they would put even this on my tab and they wouldn't reel me in until it was too late. Then, as if being punctual, I read the *South China Post* through my reading glasses, not really taking anything in. At length a mushroom soup appeared. It combined almonds, berries, purple gorse flowers, and pieces of blossoming thyme. On the ceiling, *stars* came on, flickering on and off like a night sky, and I drank lightly, then mulled over a long coffee and petits fours. It reminded me of a French restaurant that used to stand at the center of Haywards Heath that my parents would frequent once a month, on the day my father got his paycheck. It was fronted by heavy curtains and a menu was posted on the glass pane. Vol-au-vents and chicken estragon, steak Rossini with foie gras and Dauphinois potatoes. Here Mum and Dad sat in a window seat and shared a bottle of unpronounceable wine, hands entwined, over a pink lampshade with golden tassels, and reviewed their tax receipts as they cracked open the frozen snails *served in their shells*. Frugal and broke to the end, but able to eat steak Rossini once a month at the Auberge du Soleil on Twickenham Drive.

I took out my notebook and tabulated all the plays I had made over the last seventy-two hours, calculating the sequences of hands and the scores I had achieved and then the money I had won. I knew more or less how I had played week by week for the previous month and I could visualize it as a flat line on a graph, with a few rises and drops here and there. Now the line was plunging downward with no floor in sight, but if I could hold my nerve for another two nights and I bet conservatively, something extraordinary might happen. My winnings might run into millions. My losses might run into millions, too, but the statistical gap between these two outcomes was virtually nothing. The casinos were so secretive on this score that one could never find out what the gap actually was, and I certainly didn't understand it. I had a few amateur theories and nothing more, and it was likely that I had no idea what I was talking about.

I ate a chocolate soufflé and wondered if I should finally buy a decent watch if I won, since my fake Chinese Rolex was beginning to slow down and I felt the itch to spend some of this future cash that had suddenly descended upon me in the realm of probability. I wanted to kill it dead by spending it, like an exorcism. But if I lost—

To Hong Fak VIP again, then. Its First Empire lamps were looking sultry, the gold Corinthian capitals newly washed and sparkling. A landscape of wish fulfillment, and therefore of disciplined madness. The potted trees had been sprayed with water like supermarket legumes, and the neo-classical gold everywhere was almost a struggle to behold because the brightness fought its way violently into the eye and *increased*. I sat at a table of fourteen, mostly young and indolently thuggish men in leather or velvet jackets, the kinds with wide lapels like the accoutrements of famished princes. The rings and watches burst with Indian diamonds and they played like tycoons, though they were nothing of the sort. They played rapid hands, crying loud when they lost and won, saying prayers to themselves. The smoke stung the eyes. I played quietly, speaking in Mandarin, and I lost two hands of three hundred dollars apiece. I lost for an hour and then gave up and went up to New Wing.

There's always a way to win at baccarat if you are patient and stay cool. It's like any other game. In fact, where skill is not involved you have a better chance against the house than you would otherwise. The house always knows that most people play incompetently and without a cool head. If you play better than averagely the odds are still stacked against you, whereas if you are playing with luck alone you have a fair chance of not losing too much and occasionally breaking even. With baccarat the secret is in pacing your bets, spreading them out evenly. Keeping a cool head, not with regard to a strategy aimed at deceiving others, but with regard to your own eagerness to win. It is a different kind of coolness that is required. The opponent is yourself.

Moreover, you are up against *laws*, and the laws will favor you if you show no arrogance toward them. They will not harm you if you never assume that you are superior to them.

It was a realistic concept to a people like the Chinese, whereas to Westerners it is anathema. We think of laws as inert principles that we can overcome and manipulate in our favor. I had certainly thought that way when I decided to become a lawyer! Gradually, I was learning to lose this conception of the world, and to accept a more realistic attitude toward the laws of statistical odds. The Chinese seemed very superstitious about these things, but side by side with the superstition was the recognition that it is far more powerful to pit yourself against Luck than against a guy in a leather jacket and winklepicker boots. Humans are not as formidable as the principles of the universe.

Luck was the force that ordered the universe, and it could create or destroy you in a heartbeat. I played my first hand against a full table, and I was glad that no rumor of my loss at Hong Fak had made its way up to New Wing. The players here, in fact, were more serious and the bets were higher. I watched them pay down their sheaves of cash and then turn their cards with hard-bitten alacrity. I turned an eight and won the round. There was a low exclamation—drawn-out, animal—around the table, and the three bankers shot me an incredulous look that could have been synchronized by puppeteers. I raked in the chips and asked for some iced water. Three people left the table and we were down to eleven. I felt high and now at last my mouth went dry, emptied out like a chalice.

"Look at that foreigner," the boys muttered. "He's got it fixed."

Why they should have said this I didn't know. It was only one hand and I hadn't won with a natural.

Yet I felt exceptional as the next hand was dealt, as a shaman might who had been selected by a higher power to perform a single extraordinary task. But what was that task? Who had done the selecting?

I laid down a five-thousand-dollar bet. The room turned like something that has a rotating axis. I won two more hands. These consecutive wins suddenly induced a mood of hysterical superstitiousness in the entire room, and I noticed the tables thinning out as people migrated to mine. Success is irresistible. It's like a crime scene, something that enchants the worst side of the mind. It was a spectacle for them, and soon the word *flow* circulated around the smoky space and became a wavelike sound, a word that ebbed and flowed itself.

"Sir," the principal banker asked me, "are we going on?"

"Why not?"

"Are you sure?"

"Of course I'm sure. Do I look otherwise?"

"As you wish."

"When I say I want to go on, I go on."

"Yes, sir."

His tone was jittery. Beneath his show of concern for my risky behavior lay a distinct apprehension caused by the unpredictability of *gwai lo* behavior when Luck suddenly reversed. He glanced toward the door, through which he appeared to be expecting someone to walk at any moment. But as he did so it was a couple that appeared, or at least a man and a woman going through the motions of being a couple, and I saw at once that the woman was Dao-Ming and that she was dressed up for the night with a certain level of taste and refinement that she had not had the last time we met. She also saw me at once and her face went cold and tense, and yet it was also possible, I thought, that it was not Dao-Ming at all but someone else altogether. This woman, whoever she was, dropped the man's hand and as he went off to a table she sat alone on one of the sofas and waited for a server. Her escort was middle-aged and obviously familiar to her, and I watched him sit at a distant table, oblivious to our glances. It was definitely her, I then realized, and my heart slumped a little.

I waited patiently for the next hand to be played out, and I had a feeling that it was going to be a natural, a perfect nine.

As I waited for the cards to be turned, the woman on the sofa watched me with great interest, and as she did so she occasionally turned away and powdered her face in a hand mirror. I was now emboldened by something—by the thought of a winning streak, by the woman watching me as if with sexual interest (but it couldn't be)—and I could have withdrawn at that moment and saved myself, but all these other factors were weighing in and this is the way we are, we addicts. We can't ignore signs. So I played on. I said to the croupier that for the fuck of it I'd place everything I'd won on the last hand on this one. Insanity, but that's the whole point. The thrill is in the edge of the blade and sliding along it.

"It's a bold move, sir."

"It's just a move."

I cut open a cigar like a braggart and had it lit. The chips were laid down and there was a pause in the instruments of fate and I must admit I rather enjoyed it, because I didn't know what was going to happen next, and that is the feeling that every player lives for. Centuries of players, of brothers in arms, have felt the same.

At that moment I looked up and past the crowd and saw a middle-aged woman playing at a full table at the far side of the room. She was wearing a bulging cocktail dress distorted by her mass and a black hat of some kind stuck through with an emerald feather like the plume from a giant extinct cockatoo. I recognized her at once. It was the bitch from that night at the Greek Mythology. She was chain-smoking and throwing down cash like nobody's business. I caught the banker's eye and asked him who it was. He shrugged scornfully. "That's Grandma. She's always in here on a Wednesday night. She cleans us out."

"Grandma?"

"We call her Grandma. She's the wife of a property developer. He's Hong Kong money. He plays around with the women. She's allowed to gamble away his money. We call it marriage. It's a nice arrangement for us."

He was unpretentious about it. Now there was complicity between us: the bank that always wins and the punter who has gotten lucky for a single night, both allied against the terror of Grandma.

"What's her name?"

"We don't speak her name. She's just Grandma."

He leaned down then.

"I wouldn't play with her, sir. She's an opportunist."

"Aren't we all?"

"Yes, sir. But she's bad news."

At that moment Grandma looked up from her hand and caught sight of me at the very moment that I was scrutinizing her myself.

"She doesn't look so bad," I said.

"She's a terror, sir."

She recognized me at once and there was a cruel avidity in her eyes as she cashed in her game, got up, and waddled over to our table. The punters seemed to know her and made way for her. As she came into the table's harsher light her thickly painted and cratered face looked like an overripe peach, furred and uneven, and the eyes were worlds of private pain. She pushed her way to the far end of the table and a place was found for her. She laid a vulgar sequined bag on the table's edge and took out a pair of reading glasses, which she placed on the end of her nose. Her lips looked as if they had been dipped in hibiscus juice. There are certain faces that appear to be caving in from the inside in slow motion, like cliffs dynamited by experts. Faces that remind you that life is not what you think it is, and that no one escapes scot-free.

But in this instance I also recognized the face, as one will recall an image from a long-ago dream that has remained in the mind for a reason. And the recognition was mutual.

"You," she said to me. "I remember you. You are a bad gambler, as well as being a *gwai lo*. I have been hearing stories about you. I heard you won a natural downstairs."

The table was all ears.

"Oh yeah," she went on. "This guy scored two nines downstairs earlier this evening. I have it from reliable sources."

The bankers looked at me sternly; the crowd muttered.

"Jinxed," I heard a voice say.

"It's true," I said. "I'm having a run."

Grandma huffed.

"You call it a run."

My voice rose.

"I'm on a run. I have means."

She smiled.

"Do you want to ask the boss if it's okay to go on?"

"I don't have to ask him."

"You have to ask him."

"I have the money. I have the chips. It's all in three dimensions."

Baccarat is virtually impossible to cheat at. Grandma

opened her horror bag and took out a huge roll of cash. The crowd stirred.

"I'm not afraid of this foreigner," she spat at me. "If I lose it I don't care."

"Would madam like a glass of champagne?" I asked.

She lightened up and we exchanged a smile. I am a famous charmer. Grandma didn't go for niceties, even though she liked a bit of male attention.

"Make it cold, boys. I'm going to play this genius."

I looked over at the clock: 12:04. I was now more conscious of the time, the exact times that games were being played. As if time itself now were more carefully partitioned and hoarded. It was even possible that I was becoming superstitious about it.

The champagne came. Pol Roger bucketed in mounds of crudely cut ice. Not the best, not the worst.

"That's the way I like it," Grandma cried.

"*Xie xie*," she said after a sip.

Soon the cards were dealt to seven players surrounded by a large group of onlookers. They began to mutter the words that Macau baccarat players always mutter when they are given their cards, *tsui tsui tsui*, or blow blow blow. This is to *blow away* one point on a card, as when a player draws a jack and knows that if the second is a nine he will win and if it is a ten he will lose. Peeping at the second card from the side, he cannot tell a nine from a ten and so will *blow* on it as it turns. There is in fact a whole slang connected to peeping at the cards before they are turned and counting the number of points visible along their edge. The ten card, for example, has four points along its edge and the Chinese call it *say bin*, after the word for edge, *bin*. An eight card has three points on its edge, and is called *sam bin*.

I let the others turn their hands first and waited until Grandma had pulled a seven. She looked pleased with herself, as well she might have. It was going to be the winning hand and she knew it. I turned mine: a three and a two. At first, no one said anything. I looked again at the clock. It was 12:25. For a moment the crowd stirred slightly and resettled like a patch of grass stirred by a breeze. Their faces betrayed a premonition that had no real shape, and I thought that some reassurance was called for, some verification from a higher source that all this was not going to end in tears, but what would it be? "That makes five," Grandma said as she collected the chips. She actually laughed at it, just as the other players abruptly rose and left the table.

"My husband would love this," she went on. "He would bet against the Englishman on the next hand. He'd say no one can lose against an Englishman."

"Shall we?" I said icily.

"I'm not afraid of you, and I've already said it. You may have money, but not as much as my husband."

"I'd like to know who he is."

"It's none of your business who he is. He could buy all these casinos out if he wanted, and they know it."

"Why isn't he here?"

"Play?" the banker tried.

"Shut up, we're talking. It's not every day I talk to an American."

"English," I corrected.

"Same thing. You're not Chinese or French. Or Portuguese. Waiter, bring me a spit bowl."

The banker leaned forward.

"There's a sixty-dollar spit fine, Grandma."

"I need to spit, to hell with the fine."

She spat into a silver bowl.

"Feels good," she sighed. "I love spitting."

She offered the bowl to me.

"Nothing like a good spit."

"No, thanks."

"Shall we play again?"

I was calculating wildly to myself.

"Of course," I said irritably.

"Have you still got your balls?"

"Sewed them back on myself," I said.

"Good. That makes you the exception."

The bankers looked at me gently. I had made a mistake and they had seen it coming from a mile off.

"I like a man who can operate on himself," Grandma said.

I had eight thousand on me and a hundred thousand in the room, but I had to pay the hotel bill imminently and it was more than those two sums combined. I would have to bargain with the Lisboa management as it was, and who knew what they would say. Grandma was right. I ought to withdraw with a bit of winnings and pay off my tab with the Lisboa. I ought to cut my losses. But I couldn't. I was a swine in that moment and I loved the swinishness, the feeding anxiety next to the trough. I stood my ground and fingered the last notes in my pocket, which I now extracted, handing them to a staff member. All eight thousand. I wished I hadn't left the hundred thousand in my room; I would have burned through that in exactly the same moment. The man took them almost apologetically. He knew the smell of desperation and fever. A fever in the Congo, like that of a white man decomposing in his hammock hour by hour.

When the chips came I laid them all down in four installments. Grandma laid down large bets of her own, and our game was as slow as a very fast game can be. Her crest of bird feathers quivered just below the line of floating smoke, and she occasionally turned around and abused the champagne. My two cards were turned and there were a two and seven, against her baccarat. The onlookers touched their mouths as if they were watching a botched execution and they grew much quieter than they had been. The banker bowed to us both and pushed the chips over to me. Grandma, seemingly stunned, looked at her watch and then shrugged, as if to herself, her plump shoulders rolling for a moment, then subsiding. She must have once been a woman of considerable beauty. For a moment the *gwai lo* scum was a winner, and winners are always interesting. This lasted for about three minutes. The very next hand I lost and saw half my eight thousand vanish to the bank. Grandma laughed so loud the boys flinched.

"Oh, we're flying now!" she roared.

She turned to the staff.

"Get me thirty thousand in chips."

"Thirty thousand, Grandma?"

"You heard what I said, you morons. Do I look like I fumbled a zero?"

The chips came over. Like Soviet tanks facing a defenseless German village.

"Come on, your lordship. Open your credit line."

I didn't have one, of course.

The bankers laughed it off.

Grandma looked around the room.

"He doesn't have a credit line?"

"I prefer not to," I said.

"What kind of gambler doesn't have a credit line? I thought every *gwai lo* had a credit line."

"Not me."

"How rotten. If you lose we can only play two hands."

"I'll win."

She smiled lasciviously and tapped my arm with her folded glasses.

"You have a system," she said.

"I'm not using one. If I were—"

"You're suckering me in. It's the oldest trick in the world."

She said she didn't care either way. Money was cheap, common as earth. It always returned to you, like bathwater.

We played; I won a modest hand.

"Oh," she cried. "You suckered me in."

After a while, she said, "It's quite clear that you're using some system, I don't know what. I can't even imagine what system one would use with a game like this. It doesn't make any sense at all."

"Shall we go a little higher?" I said.

It was madness but I had to take her down a notch. She was becoming insufferable.

"A little higher, your lordship?"

"High as you like."

The banker tried to dissuade me.

"Sir, we can keep the bets moderate."

Grandma reacted strongly.

"Shut up, you idiot. You're shooting yourself in the foot."

His eyes were slightly panicked.

"Sir, it's as you wish."

"I can match Grandma."

Fuck Grandma, I wanted to say.

"See?" Grandma snapped.

"Put whatever you like up to four thousand," I said.

"And they tell me you are a lord as well. A lord. The last time I saw you, as I remember, you were at that shabby place Greek Mythology. Of course I was there, too, I admit. It's sometimes a good place, isn't it? We shared a merry look. It sometimes coughs up a bit of profit. But as I recall, you were with a young girl. Or she picked you up. Yes, that's it. She picked you up right at the table. All they have to do is bat their eyelashes at you."

I poured her another glass, and then myself. I didn't care about anything anymore. I even thought of lying to her about my system. First I was a lord, then I had a system; it was as if they were inventing me as they went along. The absurdity of the process was external to me, and so I let it carry me along for a while. And so I tried to seem calm and nonchalant as I placed the entirety of my chips on the table.

The bankers tensed.

Grandma took off her earrings and placed them in her handbag. A superstition thing. I watched the spatula move and there was a faint din in my ears, a white noise that came not from the room or from the people in it but from myself. I was dead certain that I would win right then, because I needed to win and therefore there was no question of not winning. My heart was in my mouth, beating in an unusual way, missing beats, leaping erratically, and the edges of my eyes had become glutinous and sticky. *You fucker*, a voice rose inside me, *you stupid fucker.*

Hurtling down into the pit with the worms. I held back my spit and kept my eyes in their sockets and the blade turned a six for me and an eight for Grandma, and in the twinkling of a blind eye I had lost it all. The light went out in my mind and I gripped the edge of the table.

"Grandma takes all," the banker said.

I turned to her and offered a grim congratulation.

"Thank you, young man."

She scraped together the chips and had the boys bag them.

"I suppose," I said, "I should be getting home."

She lit a cigarette as if to refresh herself. "Home? What kind of man goes home?"

"A defeated one."

"Nonsense. There's no one else for me to play with."

"But I have to go home. I have to get drunk."

"You can get drunk here. Or else, go home and get some more money and I'll wait for you. Right here at this table."

I got off my stool and the legs were rubber.

That's a crazy idea, I thought. A wonderful idea.

"Will you?" she said gaily.

Home in this case was only an elevator ride away. I passed the Throne of Tutankhamen, in which a factory boss was half asleep with a beer in his hand, eyes trained upon *The Abandoned Mother*. The corridors were alive with transactions, with sloe-eyed girls. But I went straight to my safe and pulled out the hundred grand. I didn't bother with an envelope. I was astir like a guitar string. My face was bloodless in the bathroom mirror. I told myself not to go out again, to pour myself a vodka and stop right there, sit on the bed and leave the dough alone. And I did so for five minutes. I thought of going downstairs to reception and settling up at least seventy percent of my outstanding bill, which would allow me to stay on for a couple more weeks without being ejected. A couple more weeks with a roof over my head. How quickly the whole thing had come crashing down around my ears. I had miscalculated everything in a fit of prolonged pleasure. Now I had only this last hundred thousand, and that wasn't much, it was certainly not enough, but even so I was going to spend it at the New Wing because I couldn't not spend it, I couldn't stop the electric flow of my own irresponsibility. *I'll win*, I thought. *It's fifty-fifty. I'll win and I'll come home and have a bath and pay my bill in the morning. I'll cover myself in glory and be absolved.*

It became such a certainty that I didn't even need the mini-bottle of vodka I downed to steady my nerves. I went back to the New Wing in a cold state of mind, as if a meter were running inside me and clocking up lists of numbers that tabulated and measured my intensity of purpose.

Grandma was waiting for me. By now she was high

on her fizz, and the boys were bringing her oysters with toothpicks. She looked a tad more blowsy.

"There you are," she drawled. "What kept you?"

"I'm a slow walker."

I held my dough as a kind of loose paper ball that I had to proffer with two hands, like garbage.

"All of it, sir?"

"All of it."

"That's better," Grandma said. "Settle down."

I did settle down. I unruffled my heart.

"Now we're all comfy," Grandma went on, "we can get down to some playing. I've been bored stiff waiting for you. And I hate being bored."

"Very well."

I put on my yellow gloves.

"I'm ready," I said. "Ready as steel, as my father used to say."

"Play," Grandma barked at the banker.

The shoe went into action after I had placed half my pile on the first bet. I couldn't say why I did it. I was just starting to feel lucky, and one knows when Luck is approaching. I lost. Grandma ordered another bottle, and we waited for it to be opened and dispensed before continuing.

"I love losing," she said lightly. "When I was angry with my husband once, I took him to Hong Fak and I lost five hundred fifty thousand in ten minutes. You should have seen the look on his face. It made my year."

I should have divided the remaining fifty thousand into two piles and bet them separately, but somehow this would have meant losing face in front of Grandma, and there was something about her that made this absolutely impossible. It would have been tantamount to committing moral suicide.

So I put down the entirety of the fifty thousand. The rashness of doing it released me from months of stagnant indecision. This marked a crossing of the Rubicon. Perhaps these past four years I had been progressing toward this one clear moment, because one always has to be progressing toward some kind of final moment, some revelation, and when it comes it stops you in your tracks. It might be this: total disappearance. I sat there and stared at the pile of chips and many things went through my mind as Grandma assembled her counterbet. The past came back in a thousand simultaneous images. Perhaps your whole life is a preparation for a single moment like this, and in that moment you see everything at once, the cities, the countrysides, the extinct loves. You see the grand moments juxtaposed with the ridiculous ones and you see that they are not that different from each other. You see your petty crimes laid out in a neat line, one leading to the other. You see dusty streets and idle parks where you wasted half your given moments. What did they all matter now? They were being annihilated, and I myself was being erased.

Fast-forwarding, I wondered then what I would do if I

lost. I would be penniless. Wait, there was still time. Skim off one chip and keep it to one side just in case. It would buy me dinner at least. Hamburger deluxe with fries and a glass of Yunnan merlot. I reached down and took off one chip, then two. Grandma noticed at once, and she flashed me a cruel look. She understood. Two chips were enough to buy dinner *with* a bottle of wine. I pocketed them and the banker gave me an understanding nod.

It was all over in a moment. When Grandma's victory was revealed, she simply pursed her lips. She raised her glass and shot down the fizz. Something in her still wanted to lose, to destroy her husband, and yet tonight she was out of this perverse kind of Luck. The winds were with her. She asked me if I'd like a glass, too, and I said, "Why not, I'm foredoomed anyway; I might as well get liquored up."

"Go on, swear," she said.

"*Zau gei!*"

"That's better. You'll win tomorrow."

"I'm sleeping tomorrow."

Her bags of cash were brought over and she looked at me coquettishly.

"It all looks so impressive when they bring it over in bags."

You know what they call a blow job in Mandarin? I thought. *Shooting down the jet.*

"Would you like to take me to dinner?" she asked.

I had to make a prompt excuse.

THE BALLAD OF A SMALL PLAYER • 71

"I am expected at Coloane," I said.

She looked genuinely disappointed.

"Oh? And I can't persuade you to pull out?"

"I am not lucky tonight," I said. "It's one of those nights."

"If you need money—"

Her eyes sparkled, pure mischief.

"I always need money," I said grimly.

She laughed long and hard. I ground the two chips in my right pocket hard between my perspiring fingers.

"I can lend you a few thousand."

"Not necessary," I said imperiously, holding up a hand.

I slipped off the stool and she did the same. The bankers bowed and thanked us. I nodded to them with an air of stern unconcern. I was totally bankrupt, but there was an honest satisfaction in not appearing so.

Delicately, I saw her off in the lobby of the Lisboa itself. I had no idea what time it was and the clocks behind the reception desk all looked askew, as if they were intentionally lying to us. Grandma held her three bags bulging with cash and they threw her a little off balance. She laughed and made a small scene. Everyone there knew her. The thought that all that cash was actually mine made me anxious, and I was probably capable of doing something rash. She told me to go to bed and get some sleep and we would see each other the following night. But of course we would not. I would be making other plans.

I saw her to the door, then watched her totter down the steps toward the waiting taxis. I wanted to kill her. I turned, then, and went back up to the New Wing and cashed in the two chips without anyone noticing. That got me about $400 HK, not much, but a meal at least at Noite e Dia. I started off toward the elevator to do exactly this, but as I waited for it to arrive I began to reconsider. Four hundred wasn't much to gamble with, but if I won a single hand I could double it and then play that. Within five minutes I'd have enough for food for a week. I thought about it. Why blow my only remaining asset on a single plate of fried lamb chops when I could use it right now to secure myself a week's worth of fried lamb chops? The casino was thinning out and my meager bet would not be noticed by anyone I cared about. I'd tell the boys it was a joke, a formality. All bets are accepted, even the tiniest. When the elevator arrived and the button lit up I hesitated. The screw turned inside me and I failed to walk through the opening doors. I stood there paralyzed and simply stared into the empty car. Then I tuned on my heel and walked calmly back into the casino.

I went to the nearest table and sat down within a small group. I threw down both chips and lost.

SEVEN

I went back to my room then and fell onto the unmade bed. I could not think. When I was awake again after an hour's tortured sleep, I searched through the suite for leftover banknotes. I had remembered that that night there was a casino executive party at the Hyatt in Coloane and I could hit someone up for a loan, perhaps even one of the same people who only a few hours or days ago had hit me up for a loan. With luck, Solomon would be there and I could get repaid. God knew, he owed me. There was also an Englishman by the name of Adrian Lipett, who had borrowed five grand from me a month ago and whom I had not seen since. If I was in luck, and they were in pocket, I could get something back and then clear my wits and see where I stood. Which might be on thin ice about to crack, but one never knew and it was worth the try.

I got dressed after finding a few hundred under the bed and in the bathroom and went down to the taxi rank. Crossing the causeway, I saw the moon on the water, and as we crossed Taipa the car shuddered with strong winds. It was much earlier than I had realized, before midnight, and the ludicrous thought occurred to me that I had actually slept for twenty-four hours and it was now the following night. The roads were empty. The wooded hills of Coloane twisted by, the moon peeping between tossing trees. By the Hyatt the small curved beach was alive with surfer waves and the volleyball nets swung back and forth. Chinese lanterns set on the terraces leading up to the hotel also rocked in the monsoon gusts.

In the forecourt of the hotel a marquee had been set up along with a small stage; a large flat-screen TV in the upstairs bar showed a Rolling Stones concert. The American casino men sprawled in the leather chairs with their Chinese mistresses were saying how good Jagger looked for his age, very agile, and it gave them all secret hope. Red streamers dangled from the ceilings with long gold ribbons inside them. The Year of the Rat was truly upon us. The stage lit up outside and a Chinese violinist climbed onto it. With impeccable classical technique, the girl launched into a few numbers from *Riverdance*. I slipped through the crowd looking for my fellow con men, and soon I was upstairs in the hotel bar with its balcony overlooking the cove. The Americans were now out in force. The robust men of Nevada in their Singapore suits and their Ferragamo ties. They didn't notice me, because the loser always has a certain unconscious invisibility.

I threaded my way through them until I caught sight of Solomon McClaskey drinking himself under the table with a group of Chinese, and I motioned for him to follow me out onto the balcony. The group was pulling crackers and eating a roast pig. At first he pretended not to see me but was forced to acknowledge that he had and reluctantly got up from his sofa and his gimlet. He came out gingerly onto the balcony, where we were alone because of the inclement weather, and he saw the alarming signs in my face at once. The wind was loud and I had to strain to make myself understood. I said I needed the loan I had made him back. It was a sticky situation and I needed every *kwai*. I said the table he was at seemed fairly groaning with goodies and that he must have struck it good at one of the casinos, though it was none of my business. I just wanted the dough back in good order. I said it in a friendly way, without urgency, just stating the case and saying it was one of those days. One of those cursed days that must always come upon us.

"You had a bad night at the tables?" he said calmly. "I hear you, brother, I hear you."

"It happens."

"Yes, yes, it does happen."

"I'm glad you understand."

"But the thing is, it's not the perfect moment at my end either. Don't be deceived by the table. That's old man Hong's tab and I'm just sitting in. See? I had a pretty rocky night myself. I went to the Venetian and made a pig's dinner out of it. The old woman's screaming at me for losing so much money. I wasn't expecting this, as you can imagine. We all thought you were flying high. What happened anyway?"

"Never mind that. I need some *kwai*."

A panicked look came over him.

"I never come to parties with wads of cash. Not that I have wads of cash. But even if I did I wouldn't come to a party like this with it. I'd be too afraid I'd spend it all on women."

"Solomon, just give me half what you have down there. Don't be a prick about it. Don't make me empty your pockets."

"I don't mind emptying my pockets," he retorted proudly.

But he would never do it.

"Just five hundred," I said.

"I can't, I only have three."

"One fifty?"

My voice went high-wire.

"I could give you the three," he tried, sensing it would be bad if he didn't.

"You'd better because I don't have anything for the cab home."

"Jesus, Lord Doyle. You've really crashed?"

"Crashed and flamed. You know that feeling, don't you?"

"Yeah, I guess I do."

He felt in his pockets. I knew that the notes he had there were too big to take out without blowing his ruse, so he had to find another ruse.

"Let me get you a drink," he said. "I'll be right back out. What'll you have?"

"Bloody Mary."

"I'll make it lethal."

I waited, furious and impotent, and through the glass doors I kept an eye out for Lipett, he of many unpaid obligations. I was going nowhere on this quest for a repay, but I had nowhere else to go and I had to keep at it. After a short age Solomon returned with two Bloody Marys and we proceeded to down them too quickly while I tried to think of a way out of my mess and he tried to think of a way to give me as little money as possible.

"How bad is it?" he asked.

"My luck ran out."

"All of it?"

"All of it."

"Are you going to make a run for it?"

"Where would I go?"

He shrugged.

"Mongolia?"

"I haven't paid the hotel bill. They'd come and get me. The *Chinese* would come and get me."

"I see what you mean. Nasty."

"I have to play my way out of it."

"Play your way out of it?"

"Yeah," I said, "I have to play my way out of it. There's nothing else for it."

"You can't play your way out of it."

"Why not? I played my way into it, didn't I?"

Inescapable logic.

"But what if you lose the next round?"

It was occurring to him that our positions had merely reversed, and that now it was I who was going to play the money he would be giving me. Neither of us could remember whose money it actually was, or had been originally. It was just money, like fluids passing between animals. It was eternal, while we were anything but.

"I am not going to lose the next round. If I do, I'll disappear."

He laughed.

"You'll disappear?"

"I might. Why not?"

"Nothing rash, eh, Freddy?"

He fumbled in his pocket. His voice broke a little and I must have appeared as desperate as I actually was.

"Can't you pay back five grand now?" I said tensely. "I

need it to get through the next few days. The next few days are going to be hard."

"Five thousand won't get you anywhere."

"I know, but you owe it."

"How about two?"

"Three fifty."

"Three. All right, three. It's breaking my back, though."

"Those tarts in there cost more than that for a half hour."

The three grand came out and was passed over like heroin that mustn't be seen.

"It'll keep me alive for two days," I said.

"You're not going to play it?"

"I'm going to eat, that's all."

And it was true. At that point, anyway.

"Then you can take me to dinner at Fernando's. We can walk there."

"But I just bought you dinner the other night."

"You had the money. Just like you have it now."

"You gave me everything?"

"Absolutely everything."

"You're a damn liar."

"I'm not emptying my pockets for you, but it's damn true."

"You're worse than those pigs in there."

He turned and glanced through the window.

"It's funny to think," he said, "that it's we who finance them."

"It doesn't matter. I can pay for dinner, I guess."

"Doyle, it's just Fernando's. I'm not suggesting anywhere fancy."

"So you say."

We went downstairs and the cigar smoke got into my lungs and the sight of the Chinese violinist made me want to stay a little longer. I must have been deluded to think that I could belong to this world. Who was I? The insect at the bottom of the glass. Chinese crime bosses fed at a tureen of punch that a girl in satin doled out with a silver cup, and they picked the slices of orange out of their glasses with wet fingers. Red plastic lions stood under the lights, and I walked past them thinking of my three thousand and what I could use it for before all the lights in my life went out with a bang.

Solomon led the way confidently. He lit up a cigar when we were out of the wind. The path down to the beach hissed with tormented junipers.

"I don't even know why I came out tonight," he said nonchalantly, the burning end of the cigar lighting the way. "I thought I'd pick up a girl and then I didn't. One of them said I was a miser."

"So you are."

"Broke, but not miserly."

"Clearly, you're not broke."

We stepped onto the sand. The lights of the village at the far end were clear, and we went toward them, through the whipped nets and along the edge of the angry surf. Fernando's was crowded with Macanese families, and we took our place at the back of the room far from the TV sets and launched into plates of *baccalau asado* and bottles of Perequita.

Solomon tucked a napkin into his shirt and declared his sympathy for the Portuguese working class who had created this place but who now no longer existed in Asia. Too bad for them. He tore through our first bottle and promptly ordered a second. I tried to restrain him, thinking nervously of the dent it would make in my three grand, but of course the whole point was to make a considerable dent in my three grand. He drank in great, fluid drafts, as if the wine didn't matter so much as arriving at a point on the further side of it. As he got tipsier he confessed to his own losses during the previous week, and then to a small rebound on the weekend.

"And the most fantastic thing is the dreams I've been having these last few nights. The ghosts are trying to speak to me."

"Are they?"

"Yes. I had a dream I was driving with two gamblers through a village in Spain. We weren't gambling. We were eating and drinking and looking for a parking spot. Suddenly these helicopter drones came out of nowhere with white plastic propellers and followed us to a dingy café somewhere. We sat down and the drones disappeared and the old men started singing ancient songs in Spanish. Then all the lights in the village came on. I have no idea what it means. I think it means my bad luck is about to change."

He raised a hand.

"Waiter, another bottle."

"Solomon, that's the third bottle."

"So what? You're paying. We need to celebrate your crash to earth. Your imminent flight to Mongolia. I may never see you again."

"It's not a joking matter."

"How are you going to pay the rent? Don't complain to me about the bill until you know how to pay the rent."

"I have to win again."

"But you were flying high for a while there."

"We're always flying high for a while, aren't we? I should have quit while I was ahead. The problem was—"

"You weren't far enough ahead to quit."

"That's just it."

He exhaled.

"One is never far enough ahead to quit."

"And the thing is," I went on, "I do want to quit. I need to make my pile and quit. All I think about is quitting."

"You'd never quit."

"Seriously, I would. I have to."

"We all think that. Like we said before."

After an unpleasant pause, he said, "Where would you go?"

"I don't know. The mainland. One has to find a spot to die."

"You're not ready to die. You've got a chapter left in you."

"A chapter?"

"A few lines anyway."

I gave in, and I stopped worrying about the three grand. We ordered more dishes. Oysters, onion rings, late-night clam dim sum, sardines. We ordered grappa and flan. Solomon suggested that we finish the whole bottle of grappa. Behind my eyes the tears were beginning to well up, to dribble down into my nose, but I held them back and kept up with him. It had occurred to me that I might be arrested on my arrival back at the Lisboa. Arrested and deported. It happens all the time to gamblers down on their luck.

"I just saw a terrible thing in the newspaper," Solomon said. "In Bangkok, a head was found dangling by a nylon hiking rope from the Rama VIII Bridge, loosely attached to a white plastic bag. There was a picture of it in the *Bangkok Post*. A human head swaying in the wind, with a crowd on the bridge looking down in disbelief. It was a Caucasian head, and the tabloids were full of rumors about it being a mafia hit. But then it seems the forensics people determined that a fifty-three-year-old Italian architect down on his luck had been thrown out of a cheap hotel nearby, had stomach cancer, and had decided to hang himself. But he was slightly overweight, and the force of his fall had severed the head from his body, leaving the head swaying at the end of the rope with the plastic bag, a nightmarish end, they said, for a man of great sensitivity and cultural tastes, who had once worked with the great Milanese architect Cacciarli. His friends in Italy mourned him, but no one knew what he was doing in Asia. He was penniless. His passport showed that he was drifting from country to country, impelled, his friends said, by a love of Eastern art. You should take a look at that head swinging on a rope before you decide to disappear."

"What would it tell me?"

"It would tell you wait a little longer. You don't have stomach cancer like poor old Maurizio Tesadori. You're not at the end of your rope."

"But I am," I said bluntly. "I am at the end of my rope."

"No you're not. The night is long and young. If you have a thousand left after dinner, go and try a bet at Fortuna. The boys say it's been paying out very nicely this week."

"I can't spent my last thousand there. Are you nuts?"

"Of course you can. You'll win. And what difference

does it make if you don't spend it? It isn't enough for anything."

"Especially after six bottles of grappa."

"Keep your voice down, your lordship. Appearances. Let's have a cigar and lie down on the beach like homeless people. They never call the police. The grappa has calmed you down. It's been useful."

We went out into the turbulent night, where everything seemed to be in motion because of the winds. Branches and tin cans rolling across the sands and striking the walls and the volleyball nets halfway to being ruined. I had forgotten nature for months, living in the interior world of the casino, in the system of cards and cash. Now it was a shock to feel the sea air and the light of the moon unmediated by electric light and neon and the allure of sex.

I laid myself out on the sand and Solomon lay skeptical beside me. We talked about our fathers, whom neither of us had known very well, and both of them it seemed had been unlucky. Unlucky men breed unlucky men. Solomon seemed undisturbed by anything in life, neither good luck nor bad, not even the bad luck of his father, who had flown planes for Continental and lost all three of his wives to alcoholism. It rolled off Solomon and in the end it was the same. Like America, he said, he would die in a pauper's grave and he didn't mind. Someone had to die in paupers' graves. Just not a pauper's grave in China, where no one understood the nobility of being a pauper in the first place.

His debts had risen to over a million in Hong Kong dollars and his wife had bailed him out and forced him to sign a contract under which he would never gamble again, but of course it had done no good. Addiction is fate. We were the same in that respect, and the unluckiness of my own father seemed reassuring when it was counterweighed by his story. My father, dutiful and doomed till the end, a marcher to other people's brass tunes who had marched right along into a foolish early grave.

"Tomorrow," he said, "I am going to play all day at the Venetian and win back the hundred thousand I lost last week. Wait and see."

It was clear he wanted to go back to the Hyatt party, which would run late, with girls and coke and other amusements, without which, he added, life would be quite unbearable. What he wanted from it I couldn't say, but I would have to let him go and get whatever it was. The pleasures of life and flesh, the small advantages of the popular man. I couldn't blame him. We walked back to the hotel. The sound of *Riverdance* did not calm my anxieties. For a moment I was tempted to try to find the elusive Adrian Lipett again, but I knew in advance now that he would evade me with his customary skill and that I would be made a fool of. I was beginning to feel shabby, a tramp at the feast of others, and as soon as one feels this way one has to beat a retreat into the shadows. I found a cab outside the main door and Solomon embraced me. Was I sure I didn't want to come in? "To do what," I asked. "To salivate for the things on the far side of the glass?"

"I see your point," he laughed.

I was back in Macau within half an hour, and with nothing better to do I decided to go to the movies and think it all over. By dawn I would have a decision, and after that I would sail into nothingness. What was left to me now wasn't enough to gamble anyway.

EIGHT

I went to a bar near the Landmark, and I set out to get myself into the calm neutrality of total intoxication achieved through Chinese brandy. The bar was called Jilted and there was a kind of shooting range at its far end where patrons could pin up images of their ex-lovers and throw beer glasses at them. A sobbing Russian girl was doing just that. I let the memory of Dao-Ming flood back into me and soon there was very little of that memory. Through the darkened windows the first glimmers of dawn were bouncing off the metallic sides of the streets, off the windows covered with stickers and the shutters of the computer stores, and the stale odor of all the spent nights seeped back into my head and made it ache. I wondered if I should go back to the hotel and get a shot of free vodka from the mini-bar that I hadn't paid for, and on reflection that seemed like a pretty fine idea since the shots at Jilted were not the cheapest. There was nowhere else to go and I had the wild idea finally that I might collect my things—as if I had *things*—and then go down to the ferry terminal and cross over to the Hong Kong side. No reason. Just because it was something to do.

When I got back to the Lisboa the receptionists didn't even look up as I walked in, and I went up to my room unremarked upon. I stayed there for less than five minutes, collecting a few items, such as a wristwatch and a light raincoat, leaving my passport in the desk drawer where it had lain undisturbed for months. I closed the curtains and left the bathroom light on but extinguished the others. I stood for a moment in the center of the room and looked around this ridiculous habitat that I had made my own for so long, wondering if it were even possible now to simply walk out as if it were a stage prop that could be discarded. I turned and decided not to think about it. In my raincoat and suede shoes I went back down to the lobby, hoping I could pass out of the building as anonymously as I had just entered it. And indeed no one noticed me.

I walked to the terminal. A sullen crowd had already gathered for the first boat over and the men were smoking. The skies had grown overcast, and for a while it looked as if there might be a last-minute decision about whether to let the hydrofoil out into open sea. On the horizon the monsoons hovered. At six thirty we began to board, and I sat at the front of the craft among the old people wrapped up to the eyeballs as if it were the dead of a European winter, and off we set, the all-night low rollers and a few of the cleaning staff and some confused tourists and Lord Doyle, rocking on ominous swells and swinging into view of the green mountains of the South China Sea, which are always as soft and definite as monuments carved out of jade.

I sat against the window and thought back over the sequences of my losses, struck by a sort of disbelief in them because they went, I thought, against the statistical law of odds. I had been duped, but there was no going back.

Buddhists believe that the afterlife is divided into six realms. There is the realm of *devas*, or blissful gods; the realm of animals and that of humans; the domain of the *asura* demi-gods; and of *preta*, or hungry ghosts. Below them all lies the realm of *naraka*, or Hell.

Each realm reflects the actions of a previous life. People who are reborn as hungry ghosts were strongly acquisitive, driven by desire. Their insatiable needs are symbolized by their long necks and swollen bellies. Continually suffering from hunger and thirst, they cannot sate or slake either craving. They are supernatural beings and so their sufferings far exceed our own. Their hunger is a thousand times more intense than ours, and so is their thirst.

For the Chinese the realm of the hungry ghosts is similar to Hell in the Christian world. Its inhabitants have mouths the size of needle eyes, and stomachs as large as caves. Taoists believe that the hungry ghosts did not find in life what they needed to survive. They are the ghosts of suicides and those who have suffered a violent death.

And they are awaiting reincarnation, like everyone else. "The Sutra on the Ghosts Questioning Mu-lien" describes a deceitful diviner being reborn as a hungry ghost for several lifetimes. During the seventh lunar month of the Chinese calendar, the hungry ghosts are let out of Hell and roam freely seeking food and entertainment, and the Hungry Ghost Festival welcomes them. The sacrificial altars house the bodhisattva Ksitigarbha, offering plates of rice flour cakes and peaches, and they say that it is what the hungry ghosts want to eat, as if mortals would know, when in reality they know nothing about the ghosts at all.

I was thinking of all this as I got up and walked to the front door of the hydrofoil and peered out into the rain as the boat listed slightly in the wind and the guards in their waterproof capes strained to catch the first sight of the skyscrapers. The looming crystals of capitalism that fill us with comfort and dread. I edged out onto the rails and slipped back to the rear of the craft, where there was a platform of some kind, and I hung on with wet hands scanning the diminishing mountains of the mainland, on which could be seen groups of white houses and snaking roads and little fields of sunflowers. This land that I always passed and never explored. A distant paradise called "China" that was reputed to be Hell on earth but was probably something in between. If I threw myself into the sea right then, it was possible that my human instinct to survive would impel me to swim there and wash up on a beach, ready to be collected by the Red Army. Or perhaps I would have the inner force to keep myself under water.

As I stood there I must have wavered too long. The moment came and went, and as I was going black and vibrant inside, as I prepared to step off the platform and greet a long, rolling gunmetal wave that seemed to be following the hydrofoil, there was a blast of a foghorn and I was shaken back into normal consciousness. I turned my head and suddenly saw the steel and glass towers penetrating a mantle of stationary mist, a Wagnerian spectacle of pure horror that overwhelmed any petty thoughts of my own. It so surprised me that I stepped back from the precipice and caught my breath.

It was enough to spoil the opportunity, and then we were passing Sulphur Sound and it was too late; we were too close to the machinery of life.

The terminal was its usual self, a pandemonium of wild-eyed commuters, food, and tea. I walked out directly into the traffic in the rain and strode across Connaught Road. I had no umbrella and soon I was soaked, struggling between the tower blocks of Wing Lok, the Hing Yip Center and the Tung Hip and the Mandarin Building on Bonham Strand. They all seemed familiar and completely unknown at the same time, like things one has left behind in an abandoned room, having turned off the lights and closed the door weeks ago. And then one returns and everything is as it was. I walked miserably toward the Pemberton and the Kai Fung mansion, a fly stuck in a jam jar, and my mind did not—as was customary—race ahead of my body, but instead trailed far behind it. The familiar British names that always consoled: Wellington, Queen's Road, Gough, Aberdeen, Cleverly. And so down in a quick bus ride to Wellington to Aberdeen and halfway down it the Sam La Lane playground, where a few unhappy brats were at it with their moist nannies, and farther on the street named, I assume, after Lord Elgin, thief of marbles. Elgin goes on and on and there is an Elgin Building and a building called the Elgin and the massive and brutal Sacred Heart Canossian at the end of it, where I used to buy an ice cream on hot nights and eat alone just because of the name. But the center of Elgin is the escalators that rise through the tenements and the tourist restaurants, none of them Chinese, making their way up the mountains toward railed platforms and the silent residential roads of the heights. The late-nighters gripping the moving handrails as they stare down into the alleys passing by. The feeling of fetes suspended and abandoned as people go home. I have always thought it is the best way to move through a city, on a moving beltway at the pace of a walker, everyone at the same speed and therefore never bumping into one another. I dropped into Taku and sat at the sushi bar dithering, and then decided I couldn't risk my last pennies on a shrimp roll. I just needed to clear my head, or drink, and I didn't have enough money to drink for long. One cold Asahi tap at the bar. The serving girls stared at me. It must have been the shaking hand, the foam on the lip. I went all the way up the mountain on the escalators and soon it began to rain and when I looked down at the canyons of vertical neon and horizontal laundry I saw that the pavement shone and the crowds had departed for a while. The wider roads here were nearly empty, the red and white taxis crawling along them with their service lights on, and the serious middle classes scurrying with their plastic umbrellas, anxious to get back to their tower blocks. I could feel the sweaty closeness of the destroyed forests, the humid gardens framed with concrete and the whir of the air-conditioning units.

I got to the last "station" and stood there under the white lights watching the young couples come up the escalators hand in hand, wondering if once I had looked like that, thin and tensile, with a girl on my arm and a look of waspish affluence. Western boys and Asian girls, children of banks and insurance companies and press agencies, couples forged by a crossroads in history. They were aliens to me, another species altogether. I gripped the wet rail and let the rain spatter my face. The shakes came on again. Where did I go from there, suspended between sky and water and laundry? The thought of suicide, invitingly voluptuous. I'd only have to slip over the railing and drop into the chasm where the pools of water were forming. Like tossing a paper airplane and letting gravity take over.

I walked back down on slippery steps. I found Hollywood Road and the bars were filled with Englishmen standing oblivious in the rain just as they do in London, beers in hand, mildly oafish and good-natured, but then I lost heart and I didn't know what I was doing and I thought: *I have to get to Kowloon, I have to get over the bay to Kowloon and have tea at the Intercontinental that I can't pay for, but I'll find an excuse and they'll let me off.* It would help me clear my head and calm down. So I turned and headed back to the water on the brink of paranoia. A thousand bucks won't buy you tea and scones in Hong Kong.

Seabirds had scattered all over the buildings near the water, and the sky was almost black with the underbelly of a typhoon that was still hundreds of miles away. I rode over at rush hour. It was a short walk to Salisbury Road. The Intercontinental had long been my sanctuary of preference. After winning at Hong Kak in the old days I used to come here with Adrian Lipett and his girls and down their signature Dragon cocktails while that insufferable bore told us how the nine dragons of Kowloon were reputed to be able to pass silently through glass and therefore passed through the glass-walled Lobby Lounge on their way to a dawn dip in Victoria Harbor. Happy times. The lounge was quiet now, the windows streaked with rain. The darkness of the day made the quietly lit tables intimate. I sat by the glass and ordered an Earl Grey with some toast, and then, getting bolder, a fresh-squeezed orange juice.

It was then that I realized how hungry I was after the night I had just spent. My eye strayed to a buffet that had just been opened for the hotel guests. It was extraordinarily expensive, but of course one never pays up front and so I decided it was worth the risk. As I was getting up, the waitress came over and asked if I would like a champagne orange juice to start my day (I looked a little crumpled but it was a suit all the same). I said without hesitation how nice that would be. It was folly but since I was gambling with the next hour and its events already, I thought that I might as well aim high. I went to the buffet and loaded up a plate with sushi, fresh clams, croissants, grapefruit, and a small dish of *oeufs Savoyards*. I took them back to the window and wolfed them down. I was ravenous. I went back for another load and on the way ordered a second champagne orange juice, then a third. I knew that the bill was mounting up, but I had suddenly ceased caring. As I ceased caring, I ceased calculating the margin by which I wouldn't be able to pay. I ordered coffee and a brandy. It was now about nine o'clock and the lounge was half filled with men reading the Asian *Wall Street Journal*. The rain intensified. Gradually the harbor view began to disappear.

I went to the bathroom and washed my face. Where did I go from here? I was walled in with steel and glass, by propriety and by security personnel. My options were limited, to put it mildly. True, I could slip quietly away by walking confidently to the elevators and leaving a newspaper opened at the table, indicating that I wished to return. But there were uniformed staff around the elevators and that would probably not work. I could give a room number and sign the chit and hope that it would not be recognized. Asian hotels train their staff meticulously, however, no doubt with precisely these eventualities in mind. It was a calamitous risk. Alternatively, I could fake a heart attack in the middle of the room. That would work, up to a point. But the fakery would be easily exposed within the hour and the medical services would liaise with the hotel about the unpaid bill. Unwise. That left outright flight via a back door and exit stairs. Not classy, but effective. It was the one thing that might take them by surprise. As I walked back out to the lounge I tried to plan it all before I executed it, but my mind was fogged and I could not work out the details. A fourth champagne cocktail was waiting for me on the table, obscenely amicable, and instead of running for it I just sat and gulped it down. And I was still hungry. I ordered some blinis and caviar à la carte.

Caviar is more expensive in Hong King than anywhere on earth, except perhaps those joints in Moscow where foreigners cannot go. I saw the girl totting me up by the bar, but a *gwai lo* is rarely second-guessed. When they arrived the next fizz was on the house.

I ate the sugary biscuits that came with the coffee and my head, unexpectedly, did not clear. I was beginning to shake, the fingers first, then the hands, and then the whole arms. The waitress came over with the check and laid it discreetly next to the flowerpot on the table. Her makeup was perfectly applied, the look in the eye like an ink pot that shines for a moment as the stiletto nib is withdrawn. When she had turned I flipped open the folder and saw that it was double what I had on me. I closed it and sat back, thinking that I had at least an hour sitting there watching the rain before they pressed the issue. The hour passed, and then as I had suspected the waitress came back.

"Sir," she said. "Would you like to settle up?"

"No, I wouldn't like to settle up just yet."

"Would you like something else?"

I thought.

"What about another champagne cocktail?"

She glanced back a little nervously at the bar, where an older woman presided as The Collector.

"Well, sir, you would need to settle up this bill before ordering another drink."

"Oh I would, would I?"

"Yes, sir."

"What about you bring me another champagne cocktail and I'll settle up then?"

"I don't think we can do that, sir."

"Oh, why is that?"

"When a bill is issued we have to see it paid before the customer can continue."

I could see there was no such rule.

"I see," I said.

I made as if to reach into my pockets and brought up the wrinkled, still wet thousand dollars. She stood above me looking down, tensely smiling, her fingers fidgeting, while I unrolled the thousand bucks.

I was not sure if she could see how short I was, and I fudged the matter by nodding and pretending to make for the other pocket and hoping she would go away. She did not.

"Just a minute," I murmured.

The Collector had stirred and was looking over at us intently. A businessman a few tables away lowered his paper to watch us.

"Do you take cards?" I blurted out.

"We take them all, sir."

But I didn't have one. I laid the filthy notes on the table and there was a ripple of unease. The girl flinched. For a moment she looked up at the violence of the rain against the window. The Collector put down a glass and watched even more intently. The Lobby Lounge of the Intercontinental was not accustomed to such disgraceful scenes. They were probably not sure how to proceed. The waitress cocked her head. She seemed to be wondering if she should smooth out the notes on the table or count them for me. It was certainly embarrassing in the extreme in Asian terms. I had already lost face. It was at that very moment, however, that I became dimly aware of someone walking toward us, a kind of human radiance approaching my squalor from behind, a measured step in high heels, the glow of the feminine.

It was like a ship approaching a wharf on a quiet night. The sails lowering bit by bit and the prow probing forward, one of those prows carved into the shape of a good-luck mermaid. I didn't turn. The glamour of the presence was registered first in the meek, surprised face of the waitress, who half-turned on her heel and then took a step backward to admit this new presence into the force field of our scene. I already knew who it was and I therefore decided not to feel surprise at something so banal as a coincidence, because there is no such thing as coincidences.

NINE

The waitress seemed tempted to observe that the fault lay with the numerous glasses of champagne I had consumed, and I heard Dao-Ming exchange a quick pleasantry with her in Cantonese, unafraid to let her mainland accent shine through. She said she would pay the bill and the other woman stepped back and half-bowed and the corners of her mouth were sarcastically upturned. Between them the women had decided upon my salvation, and it was done with a brisk efficiency. The rustle of notes pricked my ear and it was clear that the matter was being settled without any fuss, sotto voce, the waitress bowing slightly as if relieved that she didn't have to lose face.

I stared through the glass at the mist and rain and didn't say a word. When the waitress had retired, Dao-Ming swung round to the opposing chair. When she extended her hand for a shake I suddenly leaned forward and kissed its back before she could refuse. *Yes,* I could feel her thinking as she winced a little and blinked; *that's just what a lord would do, even a broke one who has forgotten his wallet or mislaid it or doesn't like paying such trivial things as bar checks. It's just what he would do even if he was a fraud lord who has become used to thinking like one.* She let it go. Our eyes met and there was a moment of questioning, accusation, and nothing was said at the end of it. It seemed to me then that years and years had passed since we had seen each other, and during these years entire lives had been played out and even reached their end. We had diverged, and I had gone downhill.

"You paid it," I said simply, and all my surprise burst out, causing her to sit down quickly and motion to the waitress to come back.

When she did, Dao-Ming said to her:

"Could I have two champagne cocktails?"

"Yes, madam."

"And some chocolates, please. The Earl Grey kind."

Dao-Ming laid her handbag next to her and opened it. She looked up at the view, within which the dark red sails of junks could be seen moving in slow motion. She was in a sleeveless evening dress, lamé touches, silk straps, something that must have been paid for by someone. It was a condescending thought, but the difference in her appearance from the previous time I had seen her made it inevitable. And then it became clear that she had spent the night in this hotel. That she was wearing the clothes she had arrived in the evening before. A client. She was not disheveled or off balance. She had made herself up for her morning exit. The hand of a pro.

Every morning must be the same. The luxury hotel, the Lobby Lounge with its anonymous amenities, the deflected glance of the slightly disapproving staff who are nevertheless trained to respect everyone but murderers. I struggled to find the words.

"Thank you. I must have left my money in Macau."

It made her smile.

"That was silly."

"I do that sometimes."

"Do you?"

"Yes."

"Leave all your money behind?"

"Yes."

"I see."

"I'm forgetful. It's a trait of mine."

"Yes, it is," she said reproachfully.

But there was a humor, too, that had its way with me.

"Well," I objected, "I didn't have—"

"It doesn't matter. Clients rarely call back."

"You're quite wrong about that."

It's the way men treat women, she was thinking, I could see.

"I didn't expect any special consideration," she said tersely.

It was a futile exchange, in the end.

"It's money that fucks everything up," I said.

"Never mind. Do you like chocolates?"

"Not in the morning."

"I seem to eat them round the clock," she said.

"But you never get fat."

"No. Nothing makes me fat."

The tray of chocolates arrived. She impaled one on the end of a fork. It looked a little strange eaten this way, and I had to watch. Perhaps she didn't know any other way to eat chocolates, or she thought it was the correct way. Her hands looked powdered. The chocolate smeared the corner of her mouth. She dabbed it away with a stiff napkin. From afar came the music of the rain, hissing against the fifteen-foot-high glass, and the streaking water cast a metallic luminosity against the granular surface of her cheeks. She seemed satisfied with her night, or the money made, and in her eyes I could see as if reflected in a tiny convex mirror the middle-aged Chinese businessman asleep upstairs in an unlit bed. She wore a Patek watch with a crocodile strap, customized for her by one of the shadowy men who had taken a shine to her. A Chinese ring with a pigeon stone, shoes with stiff bows on them. The vulgarity of the first encounter had been smoothed away by someone. She told me in Mandarin that her business, as she called it, had looked up in recent weeks and she had made many new clients in the real estate sector. The commissions were flowing in and life among the glass towers was looking up, insofar as it could ever look up in the realm of the hungry ghosts. She had adapted and she had begun to thrive, she said.

"But what about you," she went on. "What brings you over to Kowloon?"

"I rarely do come," I admitted. "I got nostalgic for the Intercontinental last night and just decided to hop over on the ferry. You know."

"So you came up for breakfast?"

Her eyes lifted to greet the view yet again, and there was a hint of green in them, of neutral submission.

"I'm the impulsive sort," I added.

"Yes, I remember."

"I wasn't losing or anything."

She shifted slightly, and her smile was slanted, foxy. I had lied.

"But for a moment," she said, "looking at you there, I thought you might be broke. You seemed to be having trouble paying the bill."

She laughed.

"Yes," I said.

She leaned back, and there was again a glitter of the imaginary eye-green.

"We're a couple of charming amateurs, your lordship."

"If you like."

I saw that a pot of tea had arrived, Dragon tea, and there was a jasmine flower laid on the saucer next to the gingersnap biscuits.

. . .

I remembered now that she had given me her card at the time and that I had not called her. I had not been expected to call her, but all the same I had not. There lay the source of the reproach that I could plainly see in her face, even though it was forgiving and minimal. Was it even a reproach? It was perhaps something else. A plain sadness at human forgetfulness and egoism. But she had not known that I had been preoccupied with the drama of losing everything bit by bit. She had felt slighted, but she must have been used to such situations with men. Things might have become tetchy, and to avoid that I said I liked the way she stabbed the chocolates with a fork.

"It's my way," she laughed.

"I can't believe you were here."

"Please."

She pushed the plate toward me.

I said, "I feel hungry all over again."

"Why don't you order something? It's my treat."

"I couldn't possibly order anything more on you. I really couldn't."

"Oh go on, I don't care. I'm flush."

The word *flush* came out in English, as if there weren't a Chinese equivalent.

"All the same," I said.

"Go on, like I say I don't care. If you're hungry."

"I might," I stammered.

She beckoned to the waitress, who was incredulous.

"The gentleman would like something else. What about pancakes?"

"Excellent idea," I said without shame.

"With fruit?" the girl asked.

I nodded.

"And yogurt."

"Very well, sir."

Dao-Ming ate a gingersnap, holding it with two fingers. She spoke with a controlled, understated voice that seemed to have found its ideal pitch. The tense nervousness I remembered in her was gone.

She went on:

"I stopped playing a while back. I was losing and it made no sense. I never really liked it anyhow. I always thought it was a waste of time."

"That's exactly what it is."

A few moments of silence later, she said, "Have you ever been to Lamma?"

I said I had been there a couple of times.

"It's more than just seafood tourist traps, you know."

It was an island a half hour from Victoria Harbor by slow boat.

"Are you headed back to Macau now?" she asked.

I shook my head.

"I've no plans in particular."

"Well then," she said. "Come to Lamma for the day. It's where I'm living now."

"A boring place for a girl to live."

I could, I thought. It was a way out. Lamma—

"And do what?"

"Whatever you want. You don't have to pay me."

"I didn't intend—"

She shook her head.

"It doesn't matter. You don't have to pay me. Come as a friend."

"I might," I said.

"I want to show you my house."

If you'd called, her voice seemed to suggest, *I would have shown it to you a long time ago. But you didn't call.*

She leaned forward and there was a friendly nonchalance in the way the offer turned into an inviting pout, a widening of the eyes, and I thought, *Yes, it might be quite pleasant after all, a few days in Lamma while I extricate myself from my mess and decide what to do.* The sexual offer was muted, but it was there. It wasn't relevant now that I was down and out and almost dead.

All that morning, in fact, I had expected to be dead by midday, and as that hour approached I found myself to be alive, continuing onward toward yet another opened door, and I began to wonder on the statistical odds that had placed Dao-Ming in the Lobby Lounge at the very moment I was trying to pay my bill. Millions to one against. We took the ferry to Wan Chai in the downpour and waited for a boat to Lamma.

The city disappeared behind mists. The terminal with its arrested fans, its posters for Our Lady of Lourdes Catholic Kindergarten, its stalls selling Tim Tam bars and cans of green tea. We talked while standing on the jetty, unnerved by the high waters, and she said she had been wounded by my disappearance but that she understood that gaming was the principal activity of my life. That, and not having relationships with casino girls like herself. All the same, it was rare that she liked a man, let alone a client, though she was not surprised that a man like me would ignore her. It was to be expected, she added, that a man like me also needed help. She understood that. I was sick and I needed help.

But all the same, she said, there was that irrational expectation that she could defy the odds. Life wasn't all money and rank, and she could help a sick man who needed it.

We went into the boat. It rocked already, even so close to the shore. The crossing was going to be uncomfortable and nobody was going to join us. The outside chairs soaked, the inside area air-conditioned, chilly.

She said nothing and we sat at the back of the boat, where the windows were fogged with salt.

You're sick, I thought to myself, *and you don't even know it. You're in terminal decline.*

The crew scowled; the ropes were unlashed and the boat cast off, the motors drowning out the sound of voices. It swung around.

"I'm selfish," I was saying in a low voice close to her ear, "a pure egotist. I admit it. I know how selfish I am."

"That's not it."

I had no idea how long we had spent together by now. I was surprised to see that the light was dimming even further. Had the afternoon passed? We swept out of the harbor and into the choppy waters beyond. At the end of Hong Kong island the brutal apartment towers rising up against dark green hills, Easter Island idols of vast size, a million windows dropping down sheer to the water. The boat pitching and her face pale. She gripped my knees.

Halfway across, the sea calmed a little and the birds dispersed. It rained violently. Rocky islands rose out of the mist. She admitted finally how bitter she had been that I didn't call.

"You're right," I said miserably. "I should have called."

"I didn't expect you to call. I'm just pleased to see you again."

She took my hand, and there was a reconnection that I didn't deserve. Or perhaps I did deserve it.

The boat was now moving with more assurance, and ahead the jetties of Lamma could already be seen. Isolated houses perched on top of the island hills, the water shacks buoyed on blue floaters and the glint of bamboo woods sweeping up hillsides. The village of Yung Shue Wan. The primitive so close to the hypercomplexity of Hong Kong.

The ferry pulled into the jetties area and we saw that the closest restaurant had begun to light its red lanterns. She got up a little impatiently and headed for the front of the boat. The rain had driven off any onlookers and the jetties shone like stone. We ran to the safety of the awnings, where the restaurant staff stood in their aprons hustling people in. There was a wide terrace covered by the same awning but open to the sea and riled with wind. The multitude of overhead fans were motionless. A footpath ran between this terrace and the restaurant itself, where tanks of bamboo clams and bread crabs sat under blue lights. The bay glimmered beyond the terraces and above it three vast chimneys from a power plant. A small beach between the restaurants, daunted by the chimneys, and across the bay the forest coming down to the water and hesitating among shacks and rubble.

We went along the path, through other establishments, and then out onto a basketball court overlooking the water. A small Taoist temple with the usual muddled, cozy dark red interior. Beyond the basketball court a path curved around a dried-out canal and we walked along it, running our hands over the blue railings, indifferent to our soaked hair. It led up to the village of Ko Long, the sign for which stood at the bottom of a long flight of cement steps and a banyan tree.

Her house at the top, with a downward view of a swamp of wild bamboo and sugarcane. It was a two-level tile villa that had probably been a vacation cottage, though now it was winterized. The terrace was cluttered with dead leaves and a metal rake, a flat roof and painted gutters, shutters facing the swamp and a modest square garden that she had let go to ruin. From there we could see the line of the jungled hills, and beyond it the huge blades of a wind turbine turning, a single blade visible for a moment, moving clockwise, and then disappearing.

She paused with the key for a moment before inserting it into the door, and I thought it had occurred to her that this was not perhaps the good idea she'd thought it was. Perhaps it had finally occurred to her that I was not the lord she'd hoped I was. That I was merely the hustler and fraud I'd always claimed to be. We went into the front room and I saw the tatami mats and the neat shelves and the lacquered boxes, the pillows and electric fans and the kettle. It was modest and self-contained, a room of her own and nothing more. It was cramped, borderline dingy, but it had those touches. It must have cost a fair amount in that location, and Dao-Ming had clearly renovated it herself to make it conform to her tastes. She lived mostly on the upper floor, from where the floor-to-ceiling sliding windows offered a view that ended with another island. The bamboo blinds were rolled up on strings. There were no images on the walls.

I must have been so exhausted that I fell asleep as soon as I was off my feet. The room filled with cloying steam and she broke the edge of a cake of oolong into a cast-iron pot, the tea bursting into fragrance as she broke it up. She went to the French windows and opened them slightly, enough to admit a finger of air. It wasn't cold, just sea-damp and breezy. It cut through the steam. I could hear the rain. It looked set to rain for days, for weeks even, and already it had that even tempo that lulls you to sleep. The steady quiet rain of nightmares. I remember thinking, *My pockets are empty, what if she searches them and realizes?* But she must have already understood everything and that was what astonished me. I could no longer be of any interest to her. A sugar daddy with no sugar isn't much of a daddy.

I stretched out on the tatami and for some reason it was warm, as if the floor was heated. I felt immensely tired. I lay on my side while she took off my shoes. She removed them very carefully, unrolling the socks and laying them to one side. There was a sponge, and she began sponging my feet with hot water. She took off my wet clothes, folding them and laying them down next to the shoes. The sponge dipped into a bowl of hot water and she sponged the backs of my legs, the small of the back, the arms, the calves, the shoulders.

When the tea was ready we drank it quietly. "Drink," she said. "You're dehydrated." I slept again. The wind soughed as it swept through a thousand trees. I watched her beetle-shell hair drift over the edge of the cup and then over her forearms, where the sleeves of a Shetland sweater had been pushed back. The watch had been removed, stowed away. She opened a packet of McVities chocolate biscuits and we dipped them into the oolong, then nibbled the soft edges. I noted the TV set standing on a small plaster column and the boxed writing paper sitting on top of it. To whom did she write letters by hand? There was not a single photograph in the place, no trace of family or affections, and there was no sign that other lives were present within hers. There was just the view through the window and a painting of a monastery on a postcard slipped behind the corner of a wall-mounted mirror, a place that might have been familiar to her. It must have been Sando.

Before long I was stretched out on the tatami again, now with a quilt over me, and I was sleeping long and hard, a response in all likelihood to total disintegration, the last remnants of pride and coherence swept away. It was a ragged, formless unconsciousness. Even inside it I could relish the exhaustion. The rustle of the rain and the sound of the wind rolling down the hillside. When I woke it must have been hours later and I sensed that I was alone. It was night. I saw at once a candle lit inside a stone box and a saucer of oil placed on top of it whose aroma had filled the room. She had left it there while I slept and the flame had run low. I saw, too, that the window view had filled with far-off lights, the lamps around the plaza and the string of restaurants, the cement villas with their doors covered with stickers of good-luck cats. I got up and went to the kitchenette, where a note written in English lay on the table suggesting that I was to help myself from the fridge but wait till she got back later that night before making myself something proper to eat. She was going to bring something special from the city. I went out onto the balcony and tried to imagine where I was. I looked down at the muddy road, where dogs stood under a lamp wagging their tails and waiting. The trees writhed, the field of bright green bamboo rippling and seething. The house next door was shuttered down in darkness, the windows sealed with metal blinds. I turned on the heater and wrapped myself in the quilt. An hour went by and I grew restless. I always do. I put on my shoes and went downstairs to the locked door of the lower level that she had asked that I not open. I tried the handle but it wouldn't yield. I peered through the crack. All I saw was the streetlamp filtering through onto a concrete floor. At that moment, moreover, I heard distant footfalls and I knew that it was her. I crept back upstairs and took off my shoes again, laying them against the door.

Dao-Ming came up the stairs with a box of goose eggs, some food in take-out boxes, and a bottle of Yellowtail wine. She was in a waterproof motorcycle jacket and goggles and her hair was wrapped in a see-through plastic bag, which she tore off as she laid the items down on the kitchen bar. She smiled when she saw me huddled in the quilt and told me she had bought goose eggs to make me feel better and fried wontons and other things that were reputed to be restorative. We made a little dinner out of it. I ate the goose eggs cracked into a glass and whisked with soy milk. Then the wontons. I hardly noticed the storm now lashing the house, the cables singing outside. She made us gin and tonics, with the rinds of lemons cut like fingernails. The wine was for later.

She was relaxed, which she wouldn't have been after a client. Perhaps she had not had one. We sat around the low table and ate the last two uncooked eggs, breaking them and separating the whites and the yolks into the two shells and drinking them one after the other. She talked as slowly as a woman can talk, her vowels dragged out as she gave her sentences weight, and her thoughts sat upon them like tiny riders upon horses who don't use bits or spurs.

She said, "You slept for a whole day, a whole night. I've never seen a man sleep like that."

"I've never slept like that."

She sipped her gin and tonic.

"I have been thinking. It was so remarkable to see you at the Intercontinental. When I saw you I thought—I thought you were a ghost. It was as if you were dead. You were dead and I had come across you all the same."

"I wasn't *quite* dead," I said.

"But almost, no?"

"I crashed at the tables. I burned out."

Was that death of sorts?

She took off her slippers.

"That's how I know that look."

"All gamblers—"

"Yes, you burn out."

"I lost it all," I said. "Everything. Everything."

"You have to forget all the money you've lost."

I told her how much it was.

"It's all right," she replied. "I've heard of worse."

"But other men are millionaires," I said.

"It doesn't matter if they are. They can lose everything, too."

"Yes."

"You couldn't pay at the hotel. I know."

I laughed.

"If you hadn't been there—"

She smiled.

"You'd be washing the dishes."

I'd be deported, I thought.

And yet, I wanted to say, I couldn't help myself. I was compelled.

"I just want you to eat," she said.

"All right, I will. *Sihk faan.*"

She made some soup with squid, and we got drunk on the gin. The squid so fresh a spoon could scoop it. She brought out a lemon cake from the fridge.

"You made a mistake," she went on. "It's a very simple thing to do. One can change, however."

I didn't say anything, because I don't believe in change. We are who we are; a loser loses. She cut the cake and made me eat a slice off her hand.

"It's not the mistake you think. You made a mistake thinking I didn't know. You can't hide your desperation. You don't *have* to hide your desperation."

She ate the cake as well, and she said she had a bottle of rum intact.

"Disgusting but good. Shall we?"

She laughed, covering her mouth.

"I was sure you are an alcoholic," she went on. "You behave like one. Alcoholics always lie about their problems."

"Maybe I am just a liar."

"Is everything you do a lie?"

I nodded.

"I also have some red opium if you don't like the rum. We can smoke it the old-fashioned way. With cake."

She lit another oil lamp and set it on the floor next to us. She took out a glass pipe and prepared it; we angled it against us and puffed for a while. It was good stuff, juicy and pungent, and because I hadn't smoked it in years it had the power of nostalgia. I noticed how oily my lips had become, and how the slime of the goose egg had coated the inside of my mouth, undissolved by the other foods. She laid out the sofa bed and we lay with the oil lamp flickering against the wet window listening to the cables, continuing to smoke. From down in that imponderable darkness I could hear the sea, angry as always, and the buoys clicking far out. We mixed the pipe with shots of rum.

She took off her clothes piece by piece, folding each one and laying it down in a pile next to her. There was an indescribable neatness about her. She folded and stashed everything, just as she had that first night at the Hotel An-Ma. When she was naked she rolled on her side and brought the quilt up against her chin and she asked me to tell a story. If I wouldn't do that, I was to tell her what my family had really been like, and what my childhood had really been like, and not the lies I had told her before.

She inhaled deeply and her eyes began to slink away.

"Lies are stories, too," she said. "But I don't want lies now."

I told her about Haywards Heath, my life as a lawyer in Cuckfield. I described my village school in Lindfield; I told her about law school in Nottingham. I made no mention of lordship or manors. I told the truth. I said: My father was a salesman for a vacuum cleaner company in Croydon. Thirty-five years with Silverliner Air Systems. He was in debt all his life. Died of an infarction on the commuter train to work at Bolney station one summer morning in 1979. Dropped dead like a stone reading the *Daily Telegraph* with a scone on his lap. Crumbs everywhere. Nothing left to the wife and son. Buried in Pyecombe cemetery with his parents. The Silverliner Anti-Static Dust-Buster 2070 left suspended in midair, his house reclaimed by the bank.

"Ever since," I said, "I've had a strange relationship with vacuum cleaners. I think of them as demonic in some way." He was a teetotaler, a drab. He organized campaigns against bingo in Haywards Heath. Bingo, the work of Satan! He wore ties with the Middlesex cricket insignia and arrived at work at 7:59 every morning for thirty-five years. He never swore, not even in the bath. He swept his

Brown and Taylor suits every night with an anti-lint brush, read *The Hobbit* to me in bed when I was nine, and led in general a life of honor and pride, a rock to his family and community, a true man in the quiet English way that no one today understands. A man in gentle debt merely because he kept to his word with regard to his wife and his garden. My role model for most of my life, until I rolled heavily into debt myself.

I knew I was talking to myself, and soon she was sleeping against me as if she had never been listening at all. I laid her head on the pillow next to me. I reached back and turned off the oil lamp and for some time I lay there agonizing about my cloudy future. Then, as if a counterweight, the past came back again and soon I was immersed in it in the way that you fall quietly into a nightmare and cannot climb out. How meaningless and repetitive a human life is, and how mechanical mine had been, I thought, until I discovered baccarat and the Chinese. A degree from Nottingham in something as useless as the law, a job at Klein and Klein, a year in Hong Kong with one of the big firms and then my employment in Haywards Heath at Strick and Garland settling wills (a lot of rich old widowers in that part of the world, as I have mentioned, rich and easy pickings for a smart young man). I became a secret gambler. I went to Paris once to help settle a claim for a client and while I was there I went to the little casino at Enghien-les-Bains. The casino sat by the lake with a suburban respectability and it was filled with off-duty policemen and failed businessmen, and what is sadder in the human world than a failed French businessman? It was nothing more than curiosity that drew me in there, but once inside it was a revelation.

I had some cash on me so I played at roulette, lost a few euros, and played and lost a few more. That night there was an old paratrooper who had fought in Algeria at the same table as me, and as I continued to lose—we being virtually the only two players at the table—he took off the patch that covered a missing eye and laid it on the table in front of him as a mark of respect. Up to that moment I hadn't known what it would be like to lose money in this way—so pointlessly—and this curious offhand gesture reassured me, I didn't know why. The vacated eye was sealed over with pale scar tissue, and this made the other working eye exceedingly jaunty. "It's like losing the men in your unit," he said half-seriously. "The mission goes on."

Then he said: *"Un homme qui ne joue pas c'est comme un homme qui s'est jamais marié—c'est a dire un petit con."* A man who doesn't play the tables is like a man who has never married—a little shit.

That was the beginning of it. I've had fond memories of Enghiens-les-Bain ever since. It was nothing more than a taste for solitude, a *capacity* for solitude. Thereafter I went every month on business and gambled on the side. It became a secret hobby, as it often does. I started to play baccarat online, sometimes winning hundreds of pounds a month. I became a sharp at it. And then I began to lose. Soon, I was traveling to Birmingham at the weekends to play the tables. You could not imagine anything more pathetic. I thought of nothing else. It was like a grudge. I was convinced I had been stiffed the previous weekend when I had lost everything. I couldn't accept it. And of course there was nowhere serious to gamble in Sussex in those days, or even in London. I felt cut adrift. It really didn't seem fair. I went to Paris, too, and got into the swing of roulette, a terrible game really. There was no adrenaline in it, but it was better than nothing. One only has to play a given game for a few months before it becomes second nature; I became good at everything I played, though that did not mean I won consistently. What I discovered was a taste for losing. I understood in some way that playing something well and losing at it had something to do with playing it over the long haul. But I didn't care, and I dare say no player does.

She was now awake and relit the pipe and we had another go at it, and soon the balance of our talk had shifted again and she began to tell her own story, as if mine needed to be evened out by hers. I had become a secret player inside a fairly comfortable life, but she had migrated from Kham.

"When I left Sando, I had to hitch a ride to Daocheng. My mother hoped I would help her eat, so she didn't stop me."

She sucked in the smoke and sank back onto the sofa bed.

"I didn't mind. I was happy to wait the whole night in Daocheng for the bus."

"How old were you?"

"Fifteen. It was illegal to leave. I walked to the bus station and waited there all night. There was a bus south in the morning. I had enough to get all the way south. I got a job as a hostess in Guangzhou. I bought some makeup and some dresses. Some shoes. I became good at it. I had the looks, the youth. I made hard cash every week under the table. I shared an apartment with five girls. We all cooked together. In the summer we went to Hainan and slept with old men. We worked the hotels."

But then she talked at greater length. Her father had been a welder working on hotel projects of Chengdu, and he was never home. He had found a better life. Her mother worked in the fields.

She was the only child. She had gone to school in the village, bright, industrious, and seemingly little connected to her cold, fractious parents. It was rumored in the village that the father had run off to the big city with a waitress from a tourist hotel in Litang, and it was probably true. Her mother, half-abandoned, labored on grimly without mentioning it to her daughter. In the winters he would sometimes come back and make his awful "Zhang wine" in huge glass vats. He fermented them all winter with medicinal herbs and then drank himself into oblivion. He spoke to Dao-Ming in Mandarin, and to his wife in Zhang. He had picked up some airs in the big city.

The winters in those high lands were unimaginable. Before they were snowed in and the road between Dao-cheng and Litang was closed, her mother took her on their motorbike into the hills where Zhang farmers in their tall Stetson hats and pointed boots sold medicinal roots to passing cars. In the autumn and the early spring they rode into Litang and spun the gold-plated prayer wheels in the temple and bought gas canisters for the house. They went to another temple outside Daocheng, that bitter and wind-blasted town, a place of white stupas along the banks of a rippling, stone-filled river, where the grassland was flat and white with ice. The mountains there were strewn with lines of prayer flags that ran from the summits into the ravines below and made them look like immense cakes. They could walk from village to village, her mother flip-ping her little prayer wheel in one hand and summoning Buddha to mind with recitations.

It was a holy land. In spring they would see picnic parties of monks in brilliant boat-shaped gold hats sitting in the new grass with yak herds dotting the dark green slopes. The tents of the Zhang nomads with walls around them. In the villages at the bottom of the gorges the houses were whitewashed. Their flat roofs were piled with drying straw and the windows and lintels painted with the violent colors of the Tibetan afterlife. The swollen rivers churned through them like floodwaters; in the awakening rose gardens the old women stood in their straw hats like ghosts, but their eyes were alive.

But before spring came around they were trapped in the valley. They were enclosed alongside the monastery in their gaunt, dark-brown fortress houses, around which the shallow rivers ran. The monastery's wooden gates and loggias were painted with gods and demons. In the woods below it lay the adobe huts of the monks. Dao-Ming went into the temple every day with a *renminbi* note, climbed the ladder to the first floor, and walked on the balcony that curled around the shrine. With the truck drivers and the traveling mechanics, she dropped her note onto the floor below and wished for her father to come back from the city and stay. He never did. The yak butter candles glittering in the dark never answered her prayer. She began to understand why he had left.

When her mother took her to the temple outside Daocheng, she told her that the dead were not really dead, they were merely being reborn, but sometimes being reborn was worse than suffering extinction.

"If you disappeared, you wouldn't suffer. Being reborn forever—no wonder the Communists told us it was an evil religion."

"It isn't evil," Dao-Ming said. "It's just true. Whatever is the truth is bound to be horrifying."

She prayed herself, and worked the fields when she was thirteen; she was never sick and the snow never affected her. No one knew what was going to become of her. She was too refined and aloof for the local boys. She was never going to be a truck driver's wife, or a farmer. She was never going to stay in the beautiful valleys of Kham. "I'm a hardheaded peasant," she said, "but not hardheaded enough, or too much so. Or maybe I'm not as much of a true peasant as I think I am. I admire them, though. To me, the word is a compliment. I wish I were more like my mother. Enduring."

She turned onto her back and the smoke shot up from her mouth. There was a steeliness in the way she remembered her own life. She put down the pipe.

"They thought I was haughty and would come to nothing. Well, I did come to nothing. But not in the way they predicted. I could have studied—but I was impatient. I didn't want to be just another pharmacist in some run-down industrial town. I wanted some good luck. I wanted—as we say—the open sky. I can't say whether I found it or not. I found you."

She smiled.

"Shall we have some oolong?"

It was nearly dawn, and through the blinds the restless blue of the sea was beginning to materialize. The floating houses bobbing. She filled the kettle and broke more tea into the pot. I put my arm around her middle, drawing her a little toward me, not knowing if I should. Somehow we never made the tea. Instead, we slept again. I felt the space between her sharp shoulder blades, the knobs of the spine. There was a curious swelling along her neck and when I touched it she reached up for a moment and brushed my hand aside.

ELEVEN

For several nights we walked down to the restaurants in Yung Shue Wan, and while we looked up at the three giant chimneys of the Lamma power station she fed me fine long bamboo clams and slipper lobsters colored the pale pink and green of shells served on their backs under garlic crusts. We went to the Seaview and picked out leopard coral groupers from the outdoor tanks or dull red star groupers or green wrasse, and had spicy sea snails with rice wine and geoduck clams and king prawns. She ordered me fried tofu, the famous Lamma tofu of Grandma Tsiong. She skewered whatever we were eating on a metal fork, lifted it over a raised hand, and pushed the flesh onto my tongue; we ate our selections with spring onions tossed in oil, and kale, with crunchy green beans and perfect rice. "There's a road that runs alongside the power station," she would say, looking toward the chimneys on the far side of the bay, "called Precipitator Road, and there's a Stacker Road, too, and an Administration Road. So poetic. Our island is a floating power station."

The elderly proprietors greeted her with a certain coolness, though it might equally have been some style of formality with which I was not familiar. It might have been because she was overdressed, or wore too much jewelry, but I sensed that it was not that. Nor was it because of her profession. It was something else. It was a coolness in her, too, a coolness that subtly repelled them and made them keep their distance, resentful and alert to the possibility of her displeasure. I sensed them criticizing us behind our backs. But they never said anything to our faces. I understood them. I, too, could not get to the back of her; her door would not open even a few inches. But still, one has to live.

When the first hot mornings came and the rain cleared we got up early without a word and drank oolong tea on the terrace above the rippling bamboo and banana fronds. The cicadas coming to life, roused by instinct and dryness. The blade of the distant wind turbine rising and falling clockwise, and the sound of carpets being beaten in the houses on the hill of Ko Long. We walked up to the top, where the paths turned in different directions. From there Ko Long could have been Italy, a backwater of Ischia, but silent and neat and intensely private. The path running along the crest, and then into jungles.

She held my hand, steadying my still-weak system,

and we descended a steep incline toward a wooded beach, where the shops were closed and from where the power station could be seen, its pale brown chimneys massive and scornful and righteous. From here the path, neatly municipal, rose steeply around the bulk of stony mountains, a place of low scrub and tawny rocks hanging above a tropical sea. Pavilions on the lookout points, shaded and filled with elderly hikers.

We walked across the island until Mount Shenhouse came into view and then the other little port of Sok Kwo Wan. The sweat dripped off her fingers and I could see the drops darken the ground. She was still closed in some way, shuttered away.

I thought to myself that it must have been because of the way we met. One doesn't forget such things. It was the money that had passed between us during those first hours. Money had brought us together and it had driven the wedge between us. And yet it had also brought us together again. It was always between us, like air that has not been disturbed for centuries. It poisoned us and brought us back to life; it held us apart even as it glued us at the hips. She could smell money on me, and I could smell it on her. Money, too, made us both pariahs. That was why the patrons of the lobster restaurant could not quite look us in the eye. We were outcast dogs and we had a dusty smell of *kwai* upon us. It was a smell like decomposition, I imagine. She was well aware of this, and I was sure it made her sadly unable to open herself to me, however much she had described the place of her childhood. She would be opening herself to more ruin, I thought, more rape at the hands of money, and that couldn't be risked. She had risked herself once and she would not do it a second time. No one ever does, not willingly. So I was content to take her hand while we were eating slipper lobsters and let her be. I knew that she would never give anything more than compassion, because compassion was now the emotion she believed in most. She was not the only one.

We sat by the water in Sok Kwo Wan, at the Wai Yee, and she ordered too much food because, she said, she wanted me to eat and get well again. The staff watched her sullenly from behind the tanks where the lobsters played with their antennae and the Japanese clams sulked.

"They hate me," she said to me under her breath. "Look at them. So pompous. So judgmental."

"They seem afraid of you."

"I wish they were. Hypocrites."

We ate with our fingers, scouring out the little shells of the lobsters and sectioning the humphead wrasse.

"You miss the tables already," she said coolly. "I wanted you to stay here. For a little while longer, anyway. But I can sense you want to get back to your tables. I won't stop you if you do."

"It's not that."

"I can feel you thinking about them."

"I'm very grateful for everything," I said. "You've saved me. I don't know what else to add—"

"But you're bored."

"No."

"You're bored and you have to go back to your games."

"Well," I burst out, "that's one way of putting it. Even a small player has his loves and dreams!"

Her hand tensed and almost withdrew.

"But then how will you raise the money?"

There was nothing to say to this, except, "One of the boys will come through for me. I can beg."

"Will you beg?"

"I'll do anything. I have no shame."

She bit her lip for a moment, as if about to laugh.

She asked me if I would drink rice wine. Why not?

"Better to steal than beg," she said, snapping her fingers at the lurking waiters.

"I've always begged—it works."

"I've always stolen. It works, too."

We drank the rice wine a little greedily.

"I'm a virtuoso beggar," I laughed.

"You can steal from me if you want. But you can't beg from me—I won't give you anything."

The boats had stopped moving across to Hong Kong; the sea was too rough and the piers reserved for the Rainbow restaurant had emptied out as the late-nighters decamped for the "Lamma Hilton." I noticed that she didn't get drunk; glass after glass and the effect upon her was unnoticeable. She didn't say anything irrelevant. Her mind was perfectly focused. I began to wonder about this composure, this marvelous concentration, her hands laid on the white tablecloth like needles pointing toward invisible things. I noticed the scarf she wore around her neck. It was hiding something. We walked back to the house, a long, blowsy tramp along that roller-coaster path.

"It's strange," I said, "how this storm stops and starts. It was so fine during the day—"

"There's no moon either."

I put my arm around her, and the thin hip flinched.

In Ko Long we smoked a pipe on the bed and made love. It was slow, glacial in some way, and she was far off in her mind. I kissed the swelling around her neck, which encircled it entirely. She didn't catch my intrusion quickly enough and she shuddered, as if discovered.

We talked through the night.

"You can't go back to that life," she said. "Stay with me. You don't need money here."

For how long? I thought.

"You're a gentle man. You've taken the wrong path."

"It could be."

"I can see you as you are."

"But I am as I am," I said. "I'm what they call a night-walker."

"Oh, I don't judge you. I know very well what you are.

Just as you know very well what I am. We can't do anything about it."

I thought, *I don't want to do anything about it.*

I couldn't change, I admitted. It'd be a waste of time to even try. In the realm of the hungry ghosts, no effort is rewarded.

She nodded at this, and her eyes lowered.

"It's always too late to change."

Tears welled into my eyes, and thank God it was dark and she wasn't curious about them because I would have had no explanation. Sometimes one can feel that one has suddenly lost something that one never had in the first place. It just slips out of the hand and breaks.

On the balcony behind us metal chimes sang in the dark, and the lights of the house near us came on. I could hear everything on the mountainside. She made no sound. She held my wrists and bent over me with her neck arched to one side, but not in avoidance. The intensity inside her was not expressive. It seemed to me—I was trying to *see* it— that it was coiled into a definite shape, like the metal rings of a spring compressed upon one another and forming a sort of tunnel. It expanded and contracted with small gasps and tensions of the legs, and I didn't know what it was or why she made love in this way, which was without fluidity or affection or drama. It was as if everything around her was invisible and had no weight. I thought then that it had to be because we didn't know each other at all, that we had merely been thrown together by chance, and this collision in the dark had its own meaning but it was not a clear one. She leaned back and her hair flew around her for a second, a great fan of scented and varnished fibers. She had the look of a dervish stopping in midspin, her eyes locked. She cried out and a second later there was no trace of that sound whatsoever.

TWELVE

When I woke, she was gone. Though the rain had stopped, the trees by the windows continued to drip like little taps, the eaves as well, and oily puddles had formed on the sills. I looked over at the kitchen and saw a lockbox sitting next to the microwave. She must have had thousands and thousands of dollars in there, and in the end all I needed was enough for the ferry and three hands at the Hong Fak. I could hike down the road to the jetty and take a direct boat to Macau. It was possible. I could take a bit of money and send it back to her. I wouldn't send it back, of course. Money once taken is sucked down into the maw and never spat back up again. I said it to myself in one nice Cantonese phrase: *hou yan wu chi*. Dead to shame. I was dead in that sense and it no longer made any difference to me if I went from begging to stealing, it was all the same. It was a question of which one was more effective. There was no one to beg from. Still, I hesitated. Ancient scruples baked in the oven of Western civ.

I opened the box anyway, and sure enough there were thousands of Hong Kong dollars and *kwai* stuffed into it. It was a small fortune. The accumulated earnings of a couple of years at least. She was getting ready to send it back to the monastery in Sando and make merit. She was, after all, a good Buddhist country girl and she would never spend the money on herself until she had made merit by sending her lucre home. Her instincts were predictable.

I wasn't hungry until late in the day, and she had still not come home. I sat on the deck and watched the fishing boats parade around the straits. At last I took a few bills from the box and walked down to the restaurants, where the tanks were being shown to a party of German tourists. The owners seemed surprised to see me at such an early hour and they asked me in Cantonese if I wanted my usual table. "I didn't know I had one," I said.

"You always sit at table seven," they said.

I sat at table seven, then. They brought a menu and I asked for slipper lobsters.

"It stopped raining," I remarked.

The owners of this place were an elderly couple and I had to wonder if we had dined here or somewhere else. When the old bird brought my soy sauce I asked her casually if she had seen my friend, the woman I always ate with. Dao-Ming would have to walk through the restaurants to get to the ferry. She said Dao-Ming went to take the boat early and no one ever saw her. I ate my lobsters slowly. When the old geezer came to ask me how they were, as he always did, I asked him the same question. He seemed slightly insulted by it, as if such things could never be any of his business. Instead, he thought it was more appropriate to ask what I was doing all by myself in the house on the hill. There were no other foreigners living there.

"My wife says you are hiding from the Tong. Silly. I said you were on a fishing trip. Which is it?"

"Hiding from the Tong."

We laughed.

"I see," he said. "It won't do you any good."

"No, I suppose not."

He offered me a free glass of brandy.

"The Tong will find you anywhere."

I wondered if he was pulling my leg, but the more we sipped the brandy the more I understood that this was not the case. He thought of me as the loner who came down from the hill for his dinner. It was preposterous. He said he had been anxious for my health. I was looking better, he said, and he supposed it might be something to do with his slipper lobsters.

"My friend introduced me to them," I said.

"Your friend?"

"Yes, the Chinese girl."

He laughed, as if without reference to me.

"You found them yourself. You came to the tank and

picked them out. You even knew the Cantonese word for them."

"Me?"

"We were surprised."

"Every night—"

"My wife said she'd never seen such a lonely man. Every night," he said sympathetically, "sitting at table seven eating lobsters and talking to yourself. My wife said you were a drunk. Forgive her—she didn't mean it badly."

"No, I don't mind."

He went off, and I finished the delicate slipper lobsters lying so grandly on their backs. I ate them with my fingers, as Dao-Ming had done, with kale dipped in soy, and soon I was aware of the movement of the sea a few feet below me, its circular motions, and the silhouettes of the hillsides losing their luminous definition and fading. The slowness of this fade was in inverse proportion to the subtle fear that rose inside me, the slowing down of my sense of normality and proportion. I wondered if I had missed the beat of his Chinese. But he had said that his wife thought I was a drunk drying out in a cabin in the woods. I had heard them correctly. The increasing vagueness of the darkness was inside me as well, and Dao-Ming was lost inside it. A brief encounter blown up out of all proportion by timing.

My hands shook as I scooped out the flesh of the lobster, and when I was done I wiped them down elaborately with a napkin and a bowl of water with a slice of lemon floating in it. The Germans roared. They were pounding down bottles of some clear liquor. Increasingly, my feeling of repulsion for my fellow Europeans was getting the better of me. But I went for the rice brandy to forget them.

The house had an abandoned feel when I returned there, as if it were now clear that Dao-Ming would not be coming back that night, and I made myself some tea and lay down for a while.

It was still quite early, but I was restless. I wandered about, flicking open the drawers and poking into the cupboards, playing the spy, a role to which I had no right whatsoever. Soon I began to realize that there were no traces of her at all in this place, and that even the postcard with the image of the lamasery was not necessarily hers. I turned it over and saw that there was a message written in Mandarin on the reverse side. The characters for good luck, written by someone from the other end, I imagined, the strokes long and sloppy and slightly stylized. The lamasery was identified merely as *Typical picturesque monastery in Kham*. Three white stupas at the edge of a forest.

I went into the bathroom and rummaged through things that were not hers, or even female. Ancient razors left by a long-ago tenant, and a tube of toothpaste. The mirror was frosted by what looked like a layer of salt. In the drawers were scissors, cotton balls, and some antibiotics. The towels were freshly laundered. Not just laundered but ironed. The bath had been recently cleaned and there was an air freshener hanging from the rail. The house was not quite aligned in a natural way; it had the slightly paranoid orderliness of a hotel room. As I came into view of the mirror I saw that my head was distended slightly upward by a fault in the mirror's surface, and that my mouth appeared far larger than it was, like a mouth pulled wide with two fingers to make a face. The surface of the face seemed blurred, smeared, as if it were made of a soft wet paint that had been pushed flat and to one side. I rubbed my eyes and tried to see it again afresh, but the image of my own face did not clarify.

I went back into the front room and opened the box. If it was not Dao-Ming's house then there was the question of whose money this was. But of course it was her money, it was the money from the hours spent in those hotel rooms with salarymen, the money she was going to send home. I scooped out all of the box's contents and laid it on the countertop. It was quite a haul, at least several thousand, and I began—without thinking or calculating—to roll it up in wads and stuff it into my pockets. Soon I began to balloon up with cash, and I wondered if this would make me look suspicious on the night ferry. No matter. I stuffed every last note into my clothes and then made myself a pot of tea and lay down. If she came back now I'd have some explaining to do, but I was instinctively sure that she wouldn't. When the tea had gone down and I had thought everything over, I wrote her a note. It was an apology of sorts, and there was nothing much in it. I said it was an ungrateful thing to do, but perhaps—somehow—she could understand. It was stronger than me. Moreover, I would send it back to her as soon as I earned it back. I would definitely earn it back, I said, and it wouldn't be long.

I left the note on the table. Finally I put on my overcoat, which had been hanging on the door, and prepared to leave. As I closed the front door I happened to look down and saw that she had written a telephone number on the inside of my right palm, which I hadn't noticed earlier for some reason. It was curious. I held my palm up under the porch light and saw that there were eight numbers, which is not usual for Hong Kong, and that she had scrawled them there with a felt pen by way of a light *au revoir.* Eight numbers in blue etched diagonally across my hand. To remind me, to let me know that she was there and that I should call her. I marveled at the nearness of the numbers. She must have written them while I was asleep.

I went out into the drizzle. My Lisboa room key was still inside the front pocket of the trousers, along with rolls of banknotes, and I thought to myself, *I'm in better order, I am remade,* and there was the phone number in case I fell back on hard times and needed her again. I felt she had expected me to steal her money all along, and she wouldn't have minded. I felt a little more confident and rational, less confused, as I swept down the hill and passed for the last time through the restaurants. I was sure there was a last boat over to Macau, and I was right. But I had to wait an hour for it to arrive. The moon came up and yet it rained. I could not understand the contradiction. The moon pale and hesitant, the rain fine and soundless, emerging from a clear sky.

On the ferry I stood at the rear watching the distant lights of the mainland immersed in fog changing their dimensions relative to the wider view. I began to calm down at last and I felt the cash close to my chest and I didn't care about anything but playing the next round at the Hong Fak or wherever else fortune would take me in a few hours' time. The names of those casinos had begun to reappear in my mind, whetting its appetite. As Macau loomed up—the first thing you see is the Sands casino flashing its ripe strawberry lights across the water, a ghostly wheel spinning in the dark—I promised, yet again to myself, that I would send her back the money in an envelope after my first score at the tables. I would pay her more, in fact, to thank her for rescuing me from the Interconti-nental and nursing me back to health. At least I resolved to do this, but I'd never actually do it. Even as I make sincere resolutions, I know that I won't honor them. I thought, *It's all her fault anyway. She shouldn't have rescued me in the*

Intercontinental. She should have left me to pay the bill and be deported.

It was twilight when I disembarked, and the crowds were suffocating as they churned between the ferry and the Sands. I was relieved and anxious and exultant and fearful to be back. I wanted to play at once. Walk to a casino and play, simple as that. I didn't even know what day it was. Thursday? Friday? It didn't matter, just as it didn't matter what time it was.

I walked and thought it out. I bristled with all that cash, like a hedgehog, and I followed the crowds that milled toward Vulcania, the Roman mall with its fiberglass Colosseum and its cloaked Chinese centurions, who wandered around crying "Hail!" to passing tourists and giving them the Roman salute (the tourists jumping back as if stung). I went into the invented Portuguese avenue where all the outlets were, things like Aussie and H_2O, and I just went with the crowd since it was useless to go against the flow of such a large and muscular gathering. The shell of the Colosseum was lit up with cream lights and for a moment it looked terrifyingly realistic, a Trajan's Column in front, equally real-looking, and charcoal fires in open braziers. A world made for us trippy ghosts, us hungry and foreign and exhausted shades.

A man on stilts lumbered by, dressed as a sinister bird, and I went through the crowds with all my dread held close to the chest, looking up at Moorish minarets and Dutch gables and the sign for the Camoes restaurant. Before long I could feel the cash beating like something mammalian against my nipple and I found myself filled with unreasonable joy striding into the Lisboa with open eyes and ears, super-alive, purposeful, unconscious, like a raccoon on its way to a Dumpster, like a scavenger smelling bones amid the trash. The staff, however, noticed me at once.

THIRTEEN

"Lord Doyle?" the young receptionist said, getting off her chair, circling the marble desk, and coming into the open space of the lobby to intercept me. She was in their regulation sexy-authoritarian uniform, tailored skirt, chignon, tight waistcoat, and name badge. They are dressed like the corporate officers of the future, like the staff of inexpressible hotels, and they are as quiet as machines, they glide and purr and rotate and murmur. They are frictionless but powerful, for inside their realms they are omnipotent, they are the soft arm of the law. Who can resist them?

"Is it you, Lord Doyle?"

"That's me."

"I thought it was," she went on.

"I went on a trip," I said.

"We thought so."

Are you back? her look asked.

"I am back now."

"Yes, I was sure it was you."

There was only one other permanent *gwai lo* guest at the Lisboa, the decrepit Frenchman Lionel, some sort of disgraced journalist whom I sometimes saw creeping about with plastic bags of food and chips as he sailed from casino to casino in the middle of the night. I could not be him, so it was a process of simple deduction given that all foreign ghosts look the same.

Life is a game, I thought, or as the Qur'an has it, a sport and a pastime. It's a sport and a pastime and therefore we have to play it as such. Here, the casino is our temple of life.

The tangerine trees shone around the monumental staircase and the jade galleons shone with them, and all of it added luster to the bristling, wet mouth and perfect powder of the receptionist as she intercepted me and asked me a delicate question, namely if I had settled or intended to settle my bill *before too long*, as she put it.

"The manager asked me to ask you," she said, bowing in the Asian way to excuse herself.

"Yes," I said, "I had been thinking about that."

"He asked me to ask if you'd pay it before midnight tonight, if that's possible."

Theatrically I glanced down at my watch.

"Oh, midnight tonight?"

"Yes, sir."

"Well, I could, I don't see why not. What time is it

now? Nine. Well, let me just go up to my room and get some money and I'll be down before midnight."

"Now, sir?"

"Well, before midnight. I want to have a shower and some dinner."

"I think the manager said it was quite urgent."

"No doubt it is, yes."

"He says he would rather if you paid straight away."

"Yes, well, the thing is I never carry my wallet around with me."

"But you have just returned from a trip."

"Yes, true, but I always take cash with me on trips and I make a point of spending it all. It's the way I was brought up."

She blinked.

"I think you'll agree," I went on, "that I am one of your more loyal long-term clients."

"There's an outstanding balance of thirty thousand dollars Hong Kong."

"It adds up, doesn't it?"

But she didn't laugh as I'd hoped.

"I see your point," I amended quickly. "I won't forget."

I decided to put her in an impossible position by actually moving physically toward the elevators and the Throne of Tutankhamen. She would have to obstruct me, which she could not and would not do, or she would have to insist in some other equally primeval way and I knew she couldn't and wouldn't. Instead, she followed me with an anxious disappointment at her own indecisiveness. I was a debtor, but I was also indefinably valuable to the establishment. I couldn't be enraged or made desperate, and because I was Lord Doyle and not just some commoner I couldn't be made to lose face or subjected to any kind of humiliation. I was momentarily invulnerable as I hurled myself toward the elevators with many a soothing promise (they had heard them all before). The girl hung back respectfully as I pushed the button and politely reiterated her hope, her insistence, that I should be down promptly to settle the thirty thousand. It would be better for everyone, she implied, and in this she was no doubt correct.

"I quite agree," I said, bowing obsequiously.

The upper floors were deserted and I felt I was being watched as I opened my door and even as I pushed into my room and quickly surveyed the contents to be sure they had not been rummaging around there. But everything was as it had been. I felt a twinge of glee.

I laid the money out on the bed and ran a bath. Before I dipped into the water I shaved, but I looked away from the face in the mirror. I held my head underwater and counted to thirty and in the space of those thirty seconds I came out of my funk and came back to life. But I then saw that the number written on my palm had not washed off. I scrubbed my hands again, dried them, and still the numerals remained. She must have used an unusually strong ink that would not fade for weeks. Forgetting them, I did the usual, dressing up with care, going back to my old self, dabbing a bit of musk and oiling down the locks. The charmer reemerged from the ruins and I packed my cash and walked out again into the night, wild with opportunity and risk. The only problem was that I had to bypass reception without them seeing me. This was done with a few dashes and sleights of hand and using squadrons of Chinese matrons as cover (they move like buffalo en masse, ruminating their way across hotel lobbies). And so to Neptune VIP, garish navel of my desires.

FOURTEEN

A weekend night, and I include Thursdays, is the worst time to play calmly because you are jostled and disrupted by the red faces from across the border spewing their cheap cigarette smoke. But I had no choice. I had to win at least ten thousand by midnight or be thrown like a sack of garbage into the street. Losses would amount to the same result and it was, in other words, a perfectly thrilling dilemma to be in.

At ten the Neptune was packed, the Mongolian hookers in white boots clinging to high rollers as they reached the zenith of their nightly escapades. Along corridors of grooved steel punctuated by glass columns, the night's bedraggled losers padded their way with nervous looks, as if searching for an exit from their purely mental miseries. Hungry ghosts indeed, driven by intensities they did not examine or understand. Like a circular labyrinth, the casino trapped them like bluebottles.

In these VIP rooms the bets are attractive, and somewhere deep inside myself I knew that I already had them beaten. I felt invincible, though that was a feeling I often had, and let's face it, it had often led me astray. No matter. All my fear of Grandma, even, had dissipated, and I no longer much cared if she was there or not. I was going to destroy this room of mainlanders and walk away with their hard-earned *kwai*, leaving them in the dust. No matter how much money they had accumulated manufacturing their diapers, their safety pins, their crappy paper clips and plastic widgets of the world, I would clean them out in an hour and show them how terrible the winds of Luck really are when you are on the wrong side of them. *You can make as many paper clips as you like up there in your gloomy factories,* I said to them in my thoughts, *but when you are down here pissing it all down the drain, you are at the mercy of divine forces and of the implacable Lord Doyle.*

I sat at a crowded table where there seemed to be plenty of action. Chips swept across its surface like litter, were scooped up and then appeared again in grubby mounds. I could smell the cash being forked out from those malodorous pockets, banknotes as old as Mao with their disgusting scent of ink, paraffin, and sweat. The cash that now rules the planet, the cash that we are all now forced to eat like horse feed. Bitter hard-earned cash with a smell of blood on it, the sort of tender we in the West never see much of these days. I liked the swirl and lust around this table, the way the women screamed at every outcome and the way their eyes then went hard and snakelike. I liked its intensity. This was the right spot, right in the eye of the storm. After the days and nights in Lamma with Dao-Ming, after that glimpse of unaccomplished love, this was the return to hard facts.

I converted my cash in its totality because there was no point playing by half measures. It was all or nothing. The banker, covered with appalling acne, asked if I spoke Chinese and I nodded. The table bristled. Nothing worse than a foreign chimp who speaks the language.

I threw down five hundred. The cards came slithering out and I scored a natural, a perfect nine. The chips came my way, looking sulky and whorish. There was a collective sigh, a shaking of heads, and a few of the stragglers who had been hanging back waiting for the winds to alter wandered over to us to have a look.

"There's a lucky *gwai lo*," I heard someone say, and the girls came flocking also in their immodest way. I played in my yellow gloves and the toughs gave me the eye. A second nine, and there was a small sensation. A *gwai lo* with two nines in a row? Unheard of. I looked through the tussle of bodies and saw a superbly dressed woman on the far side of the room get up, adjust her necklace, and leave the room alone.

I raked in a hundred thousand and cashed the chips straight away. Suddenly the blood began to shoot through my system and, belying long-held prejudices, I wanted to dance. The whole room stared at me as I exited with my attaché case and made my way to the New Wing, where I had not been in a while—not since losing a hundred thousand, in fact, during a miserable evening in March. My reentry was therefore very different from my last exit, and I allowed myself a bit of puffery going in, snapping my fingers for my chips as I threw out a few bundles of fresh cash. The New Wing was a place I always feared a little because I seemed to have a tendency to lose there, but now I wanted to slap it in the face and prove to it, and to myself, that the *I Ching* was on my side after a long period of cosmic disloyalty. I lost no time, therefore, in sitting down and placing a daring bet of thirty-five hundred, unsure as yet how far I should test the waters of this treacherous place. They didn't know me there yet so the bet was accepted indifferently, the staff barely looking at me until the natural was turned. A perfect nine, the four and the five flipped simultaneously and showering me with golden warmth. The bankers permitted themselves a few grimaces at this brutal result for the house, but they carefully controlled themselves and there was not the slightest ruffling of their feathers. I got up calmly and walked over to a different table. Some *naughty lemonade* was promptly brought (get the punters drunk and they'll lose quicker), and I felt bold enough to knock it back without batting an eyelid. This corner of the room was emptier and I played with a couple of mainlander dotards who didn't seem to be paying any attention, watched from afar by the group I had thrashed. My new companions played as if dreaming, as if sleep-walking, and I knew how they felt because at any given moment I feel like I am sleepwalking—sleep-playing, you could say—and no one knows who I am except a bunch of dead people on the far side of the world.

I laid down the chips and waited with an unprec-edented inner coldness as the natural was turned. So I was rolling. I swept up the gains and laid them all down again immediately, winning a second time. Four naturals in a row. I already had far more than I had stolen from Dao-Ming and I suppose I could have walked out right then and made a deal with management with regard to settling the bill. I could get the rest from Adrian Lipett and limp on for a few more weeks. But then again, it would not be enough to retire on; and, besides, when you are on a roll you must roll and roll, so I threw everything down on the next hand. Nine!

The room stirred. The banker gave me an irritable look and pushed toward me a pile of chips such as I had never seen.

Their tone toward me altered. I tugged at my gloves and I was aware of how rigid and glassy my bearing had become and how much more I now conformed to the idea of an English lord living it up in the East. In the

East, people always told me—or at least gamblers always told me—they believe in the significance of coincidences. In the idea of the supernatural ordering the natural. Jung comments on this somewhere; it is due, he says, to the Chinese having a different sense of time, which in his commentary on the *I Ching* he called synchronicity. The Chinese, he said, did not believe in causality. They believed that when a cluster of things happened at the same time there was a meaningful connection between them. The Chinese mind seems to be exclusively pre-occupied with the chance aspect of events. What we call coincidence is the chief concern of this peculiar mind, and what we worship as causality passes almost unnoticed. Yes, that was how a scholar would make sense of it. Right then, as I staked that formidable pile of chips on a single hand, I knew that there was no causality behind what would happen next. In the East, as someone also remarked, *one doesn't die.* At the same moment I felt myself flowing into a great river of Luck, and I also felt how endless and immortal this river must be. Dopamine flooded my body as I merged into the flow, and I felt invulnerable as the hand was turned and I saw a fifth nine.

I took off my gloves to let my hands breathe off their sweat. As soon as I laid my right hand out on the edge of the table I noticed that it was wide open with the telephone number scrawled across it, and I closed it at once, but not before the ink stains had been noticed.

• • •

Soon I was aware of a wildfire of gossip spreading around me, the word *nine* repeated under the breath as spectators formed an ever-tightening ring around the table, their hands lit by the glare of the overhead lamps. I was aware of the oysterized breath and the scent of gum and the precision of the gazes as this ring closed in upon me and the question arose—telepathically—whether I would risk it all on yet another hand. This, after all, is what these voyeurs are always waiting for, like people assembled under a bridge where a man in tattered underwear is threatening to throw himself off.

"Play?" the bank asked in a gentle tone.

I wasn't sure. I could see that he had noticed the number on my palm and I felt that he was on the brink of asking me to open my hand and let him have a look. A crib could never help at a game like baccarat, but there is an elemental superstition and suspicion at work here, a collective paranoia, and a bank is always bound to be on the lookout for scams. His eyebrows did indeed rise and, to forestall a question, I said that it was a phone number and nothing more. He nodded, but with a clear absence of conviction.

"Really," I insisted, but still drew my gloves back on.

I didn't want him to see the number because these boys have photographic memories. It must have seemed to him a cheap way for a lord to store what was in all probability a woman's phone number. Scrawled on the hand, as a teenager would have done it. He attended to the Shuffle Master and I was surprised to see a few high rollers seat themselves at the table.

"May we?" one of them asked.

"I am playing one more hand," I said.

I heard the murmur go up: *English bastard—playing one more hand—lucky tonight—*

"Very well, sir. How much are you betting?"

"Everything."

"Are you sure?"

"Absolutely sure."

"Everything?"

I repeated the word in English.

It was those words that made me famous that night in Macau. Lord Doyle says *absolutely sure!*

"Place your bets, ladies and gentlemen."

All my life I had been dreaming of a moment like this. Absolutely sure and filled with a creamy terror. The others were no doubt pressured by the same emotion. They closed in and their greed and fear reached a fever pitch in their faces. How many naturals can the luckiest Englishman ever pull off in a single night? Ah, do the math! Not six, not seven. The laws were against it.

In that moment I thought of myself walking by a towpath near Newhaven when I was a child. A path by the river Ouse, my father egging me on to swim across the narrow river to a rusted abandoned tanker on the far side and pick off a barnacle. Memories from elsewhere. I swam to the tanker and as I latched onto the weeds growing on the metal I began to sink, to drown, and the weeds came off in my hands and I couldn't stay afloat except by hugging the rusted steel and I heard my father shouting to me from the bank, "No cowards in this family," and there was a merry music of church bells from Piddinghoe nearby. "Fear no man," my grandfather used to say in Latin. "No cowards in this family and no losers either: recall the regimental flags, old son."

A breeze of summer rot and sea salt and a life yet to begin, and I swam back with a barnacle in my fist. The cards were turned.

"Natural."

"Nine wins, nine wins."

"Fuck!"

The player nearest me exploded in heartfelt grief.

"It's the way it is," I said coolly.

The dealer stiffened like a napkin being tugged at both ends, his bow tie slightly askew, and while everyone else was consumed in the negative passion of the moment he made a slight gesture to me, depressing a thumb into the palm of his opposing hand, a smile of wan hatred spreading over his face.

• • •

Five hundred ten thousand dollars richer, I made my way back to reception and gave over my bags after having the contents counted out for me. The bellhops eavesdropped and rubbed their hands with a mysterious gesture as they offered unnecessarily to show me to the elevators. The night managers couldn't resist a few admiring remarks. The decrepit *gwai lo* they had known only a few hours ago had been replaced by the human equivalent of a phoenix. It was the power of Luck, and since it was what their palace had been built on, they were inclined to submit to its diktat.

I summoned the receptionist who had pestered me before and with some ceremony apologized for it being a few minutes after midnight.

"I was detained," I said, "by a friend. I am sorry to have kept you waiting for a few minutes."

She, too, looked at her watch, and her face was all consternation and regret. Had she earlier managed to insult what was now a formidable client, and would her superiors notice the awkwardness of the gaffe? People were fired for less, for much less.

"It's quite all right, Lord Doyle. Thank you for remembering."

"Oh, I don't forget a thing like that. I pay my debts."

"Yes, Lord Doyle."

I took out an imposing wad of dough and slapped it down on the counter.

"Counted it out myself."

"Well, I don't know what to say, Lord Doyle."

"Just call me Lord if you like. It's my pleasure."

She hesitated. Was it a *gwai lo* joke?

The cash was grubby but it was cash. It was their cash.

"I'm sorry if I was impertinent before," she said. "It was management's orders."

"Quite understood. I've decided to ask for a larger room. A suite perhaps. Do you have any suites?"

"Of course we do, Lord Doyle."

"Then get me a suite if you can."

"We can move you tomorrow if that is satisfactory."

"I suppose it'll have to be."

"I can move you at ten o'clock tomorrow morning."

"I want gold taps on the bath."

We laughed; it is such a well-known Chinese vice, the gold taps.

"No problem," she assured me.

I wondered what other petty revenge I could exact upon her at this point, but none came to mind so I wished her a good night and went to the basement mall and bought a cigar. The *relojerias* were open and I went into a few to try on some Piaget watches. It was, to say the least, a novel experience. I couldn't quite afford them just yet, but I had to savor the way the salesmen came tumbling over to fawn upon me. I said I wanted diamonds in there somewhere, perhaps around the face but certainly not on the band. "Try them on," they cried, "try them on!" In the end, however,

I couldn't make up my mind and went watchless for my Horlicks and chocolate cake. I sat at an outer table so the high-class Mongolians could see me and lit my Havana. It was, in our humble terms, the kind of moment for which we addicts live but which I had never experienced before with such fullness. Nine times nine was a *cosmic* run if I had ever heard of one, and it could not be repeated, I was sure of that. By the same token I was also sure that it had never happened before. And perhaps I would never have to play the tables ever again. I could retire.

Just at that moment, though, I wondered to myself what would have happened if I had played a tenth hand. Would I have won with a tenth nine?

I even thought of going up to the Mona Lisa and trying it, just to remove the nagging doubt. I thought about it, but in the end I controlled the urge. It was too much, and sometimes one has to *not* know. And when all was said and done I was fine as I was. At one o'clock in the morning I was a Midas in the Noite e Dia, and everyone knew of my nines. Men stopped at my table and congratulated me in Chinese. They asked me what my secret was and who I was praying to. When I said no one, they didn't believe me but they were too polite to object. It seemed as if I was concealing a secret, and some of them merely passed the table and held up a signing hand and said *gao*, nine, as if that were enough to establish an understanding. And at length I took off my gloves.

FIFTEEN

The following day I decided not to gamble for a few hours. After moving to the suite with the gold taps, I assembled my winnings in my room and counted them out note by note, with a relish bordering on miserly precision. I then packed it all in a single Adidas bag bought for the purpose and put it under my bed. Why I did this I was not sure, but I was convinced that the attitude of the Lisboa toward me had now changed as a result of my brief run of luck and the reputation it had generated for me. Sure, they had moved me to a suite with gold taps, but good luck for me was bad luck for them, and I was certain that management had instructed the staff to be a little less friendly and helpful to me than they had been before.

When I went to the Galera for lunch there was a frost in the air. The waiters eyed me coldly and their politeness was formulaic. In the lobby the staff gave me a similar treatment, though I daresay it was preferable to being hunted like a rat in debt. Of course, one can too easily become paranoid, and I was perhaps too sensitive after the strange events of the preceding night, which could be chalked up to the fluctuations of chance and nothing more. But the Chinese, I knew, wouldn't see it that way.

I walked that afternoon after lunch to the Se Cathedral. Around the little square, the wet palms, the yellow bishop's villa with its green shutters, and the mosaic pavements with a monochrome solar disk. There was usually no one in the church but a few elderly Chinese ladies kneeling in the pews, and it was no different now. I sat there with my dripping umbrella trying to clear my head between the pale green apse and the blue glass windows, and I knew that I needed to be in a Christian place like the churches of my childhood, and to listen to the voice that always emerged inside me whenever I was before an altar. I was developing the somber idea that I was not in command of events in the normal way, and that this flow that I have already described was something I could not steer in any particular direction. What attracted me to this idea was that it relieved me of any responsibility for defying the laws of mathematics. Any explanation for my winning streak was *magical* and therefore oppressive. Either it had to be explained rationally at some point, and could not be, or it could never be explained at all, in which case I was stepping into an unknown land inhabited by centaurs, hunchbacks, and drooling elves.

That's how it is. You enter the dreamland of nutters

and you get to like it and you find it convincing and soon enough you stay. You become magical, which is a terrible thing to be. All of Western civ is against you. You give Western civ the middle finger and before you know it you've become an oriental faun. You've grown a tail and snout and you pray to goddesses. You smell like a box of camphor.

Fragmentation, slow and silent. The old women kneeling before their Portuguese god who is no longer there. I sat in the aisles to the left side of the nave and looking up I saw a bas-relief panel showing Christ Falling for the Second Time. *Jesus Cai Pela Secunda Vez.* I lit a candle and prayed for a tenth nine, a coup de grâce. I swore I would stake everything on it.

For dinner I went to the Clube Militar near the Lisboa. It's the former Portuguese officers' mess now converted into one of the few genuinely European restaurants on the territory. Around its pale pink walls lies a garden of terraces and palms and fountains, where I often used to pass my empty afternoons. To one side rises the Calcada Dos Quarteis, at the top of which is a square surrounded by more of the pink military buildings. Giant ficus trees burst through the walls of the Jardim de S. Francisco. Inside, the Clube's wainscoting and fans and dusty bottles of Quinta dos Roques were what I wanted. The staff put a screen around me while I ate their dim sum with clams and their *baccalau asada,* and among those white columns and faded mirrors I felt as alone as I had always aspired to be but had never managed to be. It was the solitude of the leper, the *success*.

As I sat there with all the pomp and circumstance of a coffee plantation owner, I was changing hour by hour into something I had always wanted to be but never had been. I could see it when I looked down at my own fingers grasping the edge of a napkin or the stem of a glass. My fingers looked white and elongated, smooth and refined, and the little hairs on their backs seemed to have vanished as if they had been waxed. I was growing more sensitive to my surroundings, my senses becoming more acute. I was sure of it. The wine tasted like the best wine I had ever drunk. The rolls were the best rolls. Everyone smiled at me. The doll-like waiters in their aprons, the girls wheeling the dessert trolleys, the government officials eating urchins with their mistresses. I had been turned inside out, from failure to Lucky Man, and the conversion made me supernatural, especially to myself.

I walked down the Patio do Gil with banknotes crushed in my pockets. Down Felicidade, or Happiness, where the whorehouses used to be but which is now filled with tea shops and windows of sticky buns. Misted banyans with dripping trailers, faces like disappointed dough, the dim sum plates salty with clams as small as keyholes. I resolved to get myself some new suits made, dandy affairs with waistcoats and satin linings that matched the stripes— more lordly if you like—and some Church's shoes in Hong

Kong. The prospect of money about to materialize in the very near future has this effect upon the mind, making it soft and dreamy and forward-looking, and this was what happened as I went down Felicidade. I walked forward into the future, where I felt I belonged, and indeed I stepped quietly into it in my slippers.

I walked around the city for an hour, and an hour takes you a long way in Old Macau. The sidewalks with their monochrome mosaics, like those of a Roman villa, and covered with black signs—shells, sea horses, lobsters, galleons, and stars. The dead leaves drifting across them like shoals of tiny fish. The center was emptied because of the weather and the Fujian temples were as solitary as the churches, the incense burners dampened and giving off an odor of flowers and earth. Down long Republica, which is like a boulevard in Lisbon or Madrid, and which has always seemed as rich in mysterious signs to me as any astrologer's den. I always pause for a moment under the wonderfully named Banco Ultramarino, for example, or those wall signs that warn of the dangers of high tension cables with the grave words *Perigo de Morte*. These things seem to mean more to me than they should. Even on those hot summer days when I have lingered at the bottom of the grand staircase of the Colegio de Santa Rosa de Lima and watched as two lines of schoolgirls in white uniforms came pouring down them under a mass of matching white parasols—it seemed to me magical in some way, a portent of something to come that I could not yet divine. I would find out one day perhaps. On, then, to the Hong Kung temple, set behind a tiny square, with its boxed trees and dark red altars, and then to the Yeng Kee Bakery on Cinco de Outubro, where I used to eat for a few *patacas* a day. I remember living on the beef jerky of Pastelaria Koi Kei, on egg custard tarts and little else, and I certainly recalled those grim and grimy days as I walked on to the far side, where the ferries and cruise ships dock, and to the tail end of Felicidade and endless side streets arranged like a jigsaw puzzle that has no master plan to unlock it. Sometimes one needs to walk while eating biscuits and counting one's own steps. I lingered by those strange small hotels where girls can be seen lounging on the lobby seats waiting for secretive clients. Places like the Pension Forson. You look through the window and you see an old Chinese man standing there with his waterproof coat and his briefcase inspecting the goods, impassive and matter-of-fact, while the goddesses fawn all over him. I would go in and be told politely that I was the wrong race. *No ghosts here, thank you.* But I could catch the girls' eyes all the same, and sometimes I would be let in and I would spend an hour drinking jasmine tea from little bowls and a delicate pot painted with dragons and making love to a sly one from Guangdong, with that skin like compacted wax. How many down and out nights had I spent in those fleapits, the Hotel Hong Thai and the Man Va, whose sign still hung ominously above the street, and the

Vila Universal and the East Asia Hotel, with its desolate fish tanks visible from the street, at the bottom of which lay dying perch in their gloom. The East Asia was on the Rua da Madeira, and the restaurant on its ground floor was alive with shabby and satanic red lanterns. Many nights were lost there. A sign on the window read WELCOME TO STAY WITH US, WE ALWAYS NIS YOU. And all the time I was thinking of the number nine.

I thought about it as I trudged down Marques looking at the waters of the Inner Harbor. Eight is the lucky number in Chinese, not nine (though a natural can be an eight as well), and I could not think why nine had come to be my number. Was there something buried in my own mind that had risen to claim it? Or was it something that had come *from* me?

On my way back along the Avenida de Almeida Ribeiro I wondered what would happen if I stopped at one of the large casinos and made a single bet with $1,000 HK. I had not considered doing this because I had resolved to have the day off. But the more I thought about it, the more I found the idea irresistible. Yes, I thought, I could leave off for twenty hours, but then again I could just go in right now and get my fix, and what of it? Just one bet. Just one bet before bed, for after all, life is short and much shorter than you think. To think it over I stopped in Senado

Square, where the dampened teenagers milled around the stores, and went into an *establiemento de bebidas* for a quick oolong. It was about eleven o'clock by then and the lights were looking spectral, the balls of white glass burning with bright futility in that drizzle and social emptiness, and I sat by the window with my tea and saw that my hand was still emblazoned with Dao-Ming's number, which had still not worn off. I suppose an abnormal amount of time had gone by without my thinking about this anomaly, but now that I considered it again I was stumped by the ink's intransigence inside my skin. I looked at it more closely and rubbed at it with a dampened napkin, which made no effect upon it. It was like a tattoo.

The numbers were 6890 0899. I had not even thought about calling this number, because the thief doesn't call the person he's abused. I'd never use it. What would I say if I did? How would I apologize? I spat on the skin and rubbed the numerals yet again, but the saliva remained uncolored. I wondered how long I had been asleep in her bed. Days perhaps.

I gulped back my tea and fought the unrest that seemed to be rushing into me, and under my tattered umbrella I walked quickly past the Metropole toward the Avenida Doutor Mario Soares, telling myself that the dumbest thing I could do was call that number. She had burned it into my skin so that I would not forget her, and I didn't know she had done it, but it was a woman's ideal revenge, wasn't it? She had used magic ink and her number was ineradicable on a vital and visible part of my body, from where it apparently could not be removed.

Halfway down Soares I came to the Grand Emperor, with a gilded replica of the British royal state carriage outside it and Beefeaters in fur hats filling a vestibule of cretinous gilt. It's the kitschiest of the gaming palaces on the island, and there is something in its kitsch that reminds you that there is more to being alive than being alive. But what?

I stopped and swung myself around and through the doors that were opened for me, and into a cool imitation of some Hans Christian Andersen fairy palace imagined by a small child with a high fever who has seen many a picture of Cinderella. I passed under an imposing but strangely sympathetic portrait of Queen Liz and another of the Duke of Cumberland, a bad-looking dude if I may say, and as I went I fingered the very thousand-dollar note I was going to use. The Emperor was not as crowded as the Lisboa, and there was elbow room. I calmed down. Even an alcoholic can be calm at the bar.

I took the escalators up through floor after floor decorated in a European aristocracy theme. Passing the British floor (horses and pale women), I settled for the Venetian level, with myriad images of the age of Casanova, which is to say scenes with swooning inhabitants of boudoirs, weeping over handkerchiefs, and of candlelit gallantries around baccarat tables. A memory of another secretive gambling city, intricate and comfortable as a large salon. But here in this particular casino I knew no one at all, since I rarely came there. I passed myself in mirror after mirror, and as I checked out the distorted face that was, surprisingly, my own, I inspected the space around me to see if any ghosts were there. In that rush of overdone opulence, it would have been less surprising. I walked through rooms defined by ebony figurine lamps, silk sashes, and gold frames, where men in windowpane jackets and outsized rings loafed about on Louis XV sofas, and soon I came to a table that looked quite active and charged, with youngsters having a ball. It looked like a party. The cards here were dispensed by a traditional shoe, and the chips were pearled and multicolored. A pall of smoke hung above the table. I sat and said in Cantonese that I'd like to play a hand, and the youth looked up with distasteful surprise at my command of their slang and the social subtexts that go with it. They appeared weary at the idea of having to accommodate me, let alone lose to me at the table.

"Okay, welcome," the dealers said, and passed the shoe toward me for the beginning of the next hand. I didn't have my gloves with me, and I felt a little out of place touching the backs of the cards without the usual intervening material. But it didn't matter. I kept the ink numbers well hidden.

I was only laying down a thousand by way of an experiment, and it was really to see what would happen with the hand that I was dealt. I was brimming with this curiosity, which was more than curiosity. I was proving something to myself—namely, that I was not haunted by the spirit world. That my luck was my own and not the gift of ghosts. Because if it was the latter I would be a candidate for the psychiatric hospital. The shoe passed down the table and the players sat back for a moment and flexed their fingers and minds. The kids looked me over. I was still rain-specked and semielegant but a tad worse for wear. There must have been something about me that suggested an overeagerness. They could not, however, know the real heat rising inside me. My feet tapped. It was caused by happiness at being back at a table. I looked across the room and saw Casanova staring back at me from behind a white mask. The pallet flipped. I looked at my watch. "So," the banker said quickly. "The gentleman has drawn a natural. Nine! Nine!"

Glasses of naughty lemonade with straws appeared on waitered trays to make them forget their momentary misfortune. I raked in the chips. It was a modest haul, and I said I wouldn't play on.

The banker said, "Very well," and motioned to a staff member to take me to the cashier's window. I got up and straightened my jacket and walked behind the man to the window, causing the mantle of smoke above me to oscillate and divide. The room was deathly quiet now as I counted my money and pocketed it. I took the escalator back to the lobby. The Beefeaters with Chinese eyes saluted as I walked to the doors. When I got there I was out of breath, burning with thirst. As I made my way out into the street I had to hold my throat. In the soft, insidious rain a woman walked past the gates, a secretary on her way home perhaps. She wore a raincoat with water stains and a strictly tightened belt. Without thinking, I stepped toward her, holding out the money I had won, the notes crushed inside my fist like a handful of trash. We stopped as we almost collided and her face changed from blankness to alarm, her eyes widening into soft black holes. I begged her to take the money. She stammered, perhaps considered whether it might be lucky or unlucky money, and then shook her head, walking on with a quick "Thank you, but no," in English. For a moment I was sure that she, too, had glimpsed a ghost standing behind me. I turned and my heart was beating quickly. So here was a city where you couldn't even hand out free money. You couldn't even make a gift of it to a stranger.

I dove into the night having forgotten my umbrella, and soon after I went to a bar at the Venetian for a nightcap. It seemed to me then that I was doing something entirely automatic, and that the night itself was merely a joke, a pretext for being endlessly alive and unreal and lucky.

SIXTEEN

As I was sitting there with my mai tai, oblivious to the gondolas and the wedding parties and the slabs of venison glistening under halogens some distance away, I ran into (after all our near misses) the lugubrious Adrian Lipett, who was there gambling with his latest conquest. As I have said, I knew Adrian quite well. We borrowed money from each other and compared notes on our lucky and unlucky casinos. Like McClaskey, I saw him sometimes at the Canidrome throwing irrational bets at dogs with names like Lucky Bride and Purple Streak. He was a born loser, but he managed to survive and he always had a girl on his arm. He usually told them that he was a baronet and it worked well for a week or so, which was enough, and then when they were disillusioned he would move on to the next, for there are thousands and unlike us they do not compare notes.

He wore a tacky Singapore suit spattered with rain like mine and a wilted buttonhole peering out like a puffed and beaten eye. For that matter, his whole face looked like a puffed and beaten eye. If he'd had a nickname it would have been the Eye. He was always on the lookout for scams. He had his Chinese girl on his arm, indistinguishable from the last one, and he was on yet another predictably tragic losing streak in the grand confines of the Venetian, which flattered both his vanity and his senses without giving anything back. He came sidling up with the girl—unsteady after a few vodkas, I imagine—and clapped a hand on my shoulder as he pulled a look of friendship grievously wounded and betrayed.

"You've been hiding, Doyle. No one has seen you anywhere. This is Yo Yo. Yo Yo, this is Lord Doyle."

"Oh, *Lor* Doy?"

I bowed for her.

"At your service, ma'am."

It immediately crossed Yo Yo's infernally calculating mind that I might be a better long-term bet than the sodden Englishman she was so temporarily attached to, and I noticed a sudden detachment from his arm in my favor.

"Lord Doyle," Lipett said, "I have been at the tables for three hours and I thought Yo Yo was going to bring me luck tonight. No such thing. She has been a disaster all along."

Not understanding, she smiled sweetly.

"I have gone from catastrophe to catastrophe. Who can understand it? Last night it was all going so well. I walked away from the Landmark with three thousand in pocket."

"Yeah, it's a bitchy world."

"Yo Yo here made us both pray to the Goddess of Luck, but it only made it worse. The thing is, you know they enrich the air with oxygen? I feel high in here. I feel like a million quid. I can't stop."

"You seem to have the cash for it, Adrian."

"Why, that's just the problem, old man. I can feel that there's a change of luck just around the corner. I can practically taste it with my tongue. You know that feeling. *You* of all people, Doyle."

"I can't lend you what you need. I shouldn't be lending anything, it's my retirement money."

His eyes lit up.

"Retirement? You're out? But nobody gets out unless they go broke and are deported. And that's the funny thing. None of us goes *entirely* broke. We always have just enough to hang on."

Life as perpetual debt, I thought. *Until we hit it big. Then we're out.*

The look of despair that crossed his face was priceless.

"Have you hit it that big," he whispered out of hearing of his blinking date. "Is it all true? Millions at the Fortuna VIP?"

"I can't disclose all the details—but yeah, you cunt,

my luck changed at long last and say what you will but I deserved it."

"Shit, shit. Did you pray to that damn goddess of theirs that they all swear by?"

"Of course not."

"Superstitious peasants. I knew it."

His fists clenched, his knuckles white with envy.

"Doyle, you were the biggest loser of all. I can't understand it."

"That's why it's called luck."

"What?"

"Luck, it's luck."

"No, no. There's no such thing as luck. You turned a corner. Look, we have to stick together. We're all ghosts as far as they're concerned. We don't even exist. Even my own girlfriend calls me a ghost to her friends. Can you imagine? On the phone to her friends she says, 'I can't talk right now, *I have a ghost here.*' We represent nothing to them whatsoever, except evil ghosts. Scavengers, opium traders, and the like. Look around you. They love all this crap, they can't stay away from it. But they still hate us in some way."

"They don't hate us."

"Look at it, it's just Vegas redux. Literally. They love it and we are suffering in it because we are ill."

"Come on, have a drink. I'll lend you."

"You will? Bastard of truest joy! I knew you were a soft touch deep down, your lordship. Gotcha."

"I am. I'm sentimental."

I turned to the barman.

"Two Johnnie Walkers, no ice."

We leaned on the bar and Yo Yo went off to dance somewhere. We were the unhealthiest-looking people there, because to Chinese punters the Venetian is the last word in swanky American glamour and respectability. Yes, respectability. It is smoke-free, orderly, spacious, and clean. They don't fine you for spitting here, they throw you out. These Vegas establishments are the very opposite of their Chinese counterparts, which at least have retained the louche tolerance of ages past. The Vegas casinos are clean and overblown, with palatial dimensions and vacuumed carpets. They are as family-clean and bright as their originals in the Nevada desert, and in them the insalubrious aspects of gambling are put to the back of one's mind. The gambler here is a child in a playground diverted by toys and games. The Venetian is the world's largest casino, and its baccarat tables are set in columned halls with fountains and frescoed ceilings and cypress trees. Parts of it are like a Baroque church, with glasslike marble floors. Painted cupolas, awed crowds, floodlit capitals. Adrian liked to come here because it impressed his dates, and because he could walk them around the real-sized campanile. A place where dreams are realized, the executives have always said, and Adrian seemed to take them at their word. He liked the Bellini and the bar we were in now, the Florian, under the escalators leading up to the Grand Canal Shoppes, and I imagine that he spent hours here sipping Chivas Regal and mulling the disasters that awaited him at the innumerable tables nearby. One's demise is always a spectacle. He looked slightly flustered now as he drained his Black Label and eyed the human glow of the tables, where a crowd worthy of the Colosseum was assembled. He was defeated for the night and yet his animal spirits had been revived by the promise of a sudden gift from my pocket.

"Look here," he said, in his grubby private-school way, the locutions of the past revived in the East without fear of mockery, "how much can you make it tonight? The lads say you made three million at the Hou Kat Club. Very handy. You can be philosophical."

"It's not true, but I can spare you three thousand."

"Three thousand Hong Kong? That's barely three hundred fifty U.S. You can do better than that."

"It's what I have on me. Besides it's for your own good. You'll lose it in thirty minutes."

"Will I? Says who?"

"I know."

"Yes, you're quite the bloody expert now, aren't you? But it's just luck, Doyle. There's nothing mystical about it."

"I could make it four thousand."

He squinted and bit his lower lip.

"I have another idea," he said quietly. "What if you lend me the money and then play it for me?"

"What?"

"You heard. What if you play the hand for me and then give me the winnings. Okay, I'll give you a ten percent cut. That's fair."

I laughed in his face.

"No need to laugh, old man."

His voice was bitter and unstable.

"That's a mad scheme, Adrian. Downright insolent. But you know what? I'm going to accept."

"You are?"

His face lit up with satisfaction.

"Yes, I'm going to accept because it's just so humiliating to you that I can't resist. But if I lose the hand you have to pay me the ten percent of whatever we lose."

"Balls," he spluttered.

"Take it or leave it."

He chewed it over while laboring through a second drink, then said, reluctantly, "All right, I'll do it. I'll do it as a favor to you."

"A favor?"

"Yes. Since you've been a gentleman about it, I don't mind doing it just this once. I'm showing confidence in you, don't you see? I'm accepting it as a way of saying thank you."

"It's sweet of you, Adrian."

"Can we make it five percent, though?"

"Ten. But you know I'll win."

He licked his lips uncertainly. When money is the only thing that bonds two men together, this is what happens. Everything becomes symbolic. Human relations boil down to their rotten core.

"You don't say anything about it to Yo Yo, understand?"

"I have one question, Adrian. If you play everything and I lose it, what will you pay the ten percent with?"

"Ah, bastard of you. So I have to keep a bit back?"

"It would be prudent or you'll lose a comrade."

"I could pay you back next week."

"Adrian, we don't say things like that. You have what you have now. You don't have a pot to piss in otherwise."

His pride was stung and he swore, stepping back and bumping inadvertently into the bar.

"Got me by the balls, have you? I have the wedding ring. It's worth two thousand U.S."

I clicked my fingers to the barman.

"Two more, boss. No ice. How pissed shall we get, Adrian?"

"Bloody pissed."

"All right, one more down the hatch and then we'll go play."

"Bastards," he said broodily, shaking his head. But to whom was he referring? "I got a ring from Cartier and she threw it in my face. Those were the days. The little bitch.

But I have the ring. I can pawn it. I'm not down and out with a ring like that in my pocket."

"No one stays with anyone forever," I said to comfort him.

"Yeah, but that bitch was one of a kind. She took every penny I had."

"She left you the ring."

"It's a good ring, but I'm saving it for a rainy day."

Isn't this a rainy day? I thought. A day of downpours.

We set off into the wilderness of a thousand tables. I was feeling wild myself, and I wanted to do something fine for this declining man who had so little to cling to in his life outside his addiction. We came to a table in the center of the floor where a group of Hong Kong girls were losing their money with good humor and Adrian, attracted by the energy of the opposite sex, sat himself down emphatically among them, though with a melancholy invisibility. He then got up and gave the seat to me, remembering our arrangement.

"It feels lucky to me," he whispered. "I can feel the vibe."

The bankers didn't recognize me, nor I them. Adrian stood behind me as a spectator and we both felt like a team of some kind. I split *his* money into three bets, much against his will, and played the first hand with a calm that transmitted itself to the girls. They calmed down as well and began to play more seriously. It was a quick hand with the highest wagers turning the cards first, according to tradition. Adrian craned over my shoulder to see what was happening, and when I turned a *baccarat*, a zero, he gave a start and muttered a quiet *"Fuck!"* I leaned back and felt ecstatic. So it was over at last. My run had run out—and never had that curious phrase seemed more appropriate. Luck indeed was like something that runs and then grows a little tired, and then falls down from exhaustion.

I turned to Adrian and shrugged, and he had to yield the ten percent we had agreed on.

"Shall we go on?" I asked.

It was a dilemma for him, I could see, and not one that he wanted to find himself in. *It's me,* he was thinking, *it's me and my filthy luck. I can't get away from it.*

"One more by you," he said at last. It was worth a try.

"Fine," I said coolly.

He gripped the back of the chair. I turned a two and a three, and was beaten handily by a girl at the far end of the table.

"What?" Adrian snorted.

After handing over the second ten percent cut, he demanded angrily to play the last hand himself.

I watched the whole thing impassively.

"The least I can do," he muttered, "is lose it myself."

And he did so, turning a terrible hand. It happened in

a split second, and Adrian's brief moment of revived hope expired. The girls laughed out loud, experimental winners for a moment.

I put a hand on his shoulder and called it a night. He rose slowly and gave me the last of the chump change as my cut, but I refused it.

"Keep it for drinks with Yo Yo. Get laid, at least."

"Cheers, old man. But I can't get laid now. I feel suicidal."

"Written in the stars," I said.

We walked slowly in defeat back to the Florian, though of course for me it was not entirely a defeat. I never thought I'd celebrate the *end* of a lucky streak as anything but a misfortune, but I did and it felt unexpectedly sweet. We went upstairs to the mall and walked around for a while to cool off, and Adrian bitterly lamented his bad luck, his lack of *sau hei*. There was nothing for it, he complained, but to go back to Nottingham and ask his mother for a loan. It was a lamentable plan, I said, and one that was bound to fail. One's mother was always the worst person to turn to in a scrape.

"I just don't know if I can go on," he said. "I'm down to the last of my savings from my bank days, and I thought that would last forever. What the hell have I done with it?"

"Don't you ever win? Not ever?"

He shook his head.

"Not in three months. Losses every night. It can't be, it just can't be. I ruin everything I touch."

"It's not the case, Adrian. We're playing punto banco— it's a game of pure luck. You're talking like the Chinese."

"Don't we all?"

"But we don't think like them. Surely?"

"I don't know anymore. Maybe I do think like the Chinese. Why shouldn't I?"

As we lingered there trying to forget our misfortune, Yo Yo came up with the look of someone who has been searching for her sugar daddy and been unable to find him. She covered Adrian with kisses and we went downstairs, back into the din and musk and percussive voices. A place where the old are not allowed to be old, where the chandeliers look like model zeppelins chained to the ceilings and where their fairy light is a gold that makes the skin itself look metallic. A mix of human voices and the string music of Europe, and actors dressed as characters from the operas of Puccini wandering about in their costumes breaking out into arias or ringing bells and turning cartwheels among the Taiwanese tourists who are so anxious to capture them on film. Look, a Pulcinello. A Bohemian. Flesh turned to metal and air and pedigree. Adrian turned to me while Yo Yo went to the bathroom, and he had grasped the poisoned nettle of his situation with a shocking clairvoyance.

"Doyle, lend me another four thousand for the rest of the week. I won't play it, I swear. I'll use it to entertain Yo Yo. You don't know how demanding she is. She eats money like a badger eats grass. She's insatiable. She sucks everything up and then demands more. She's like a house-wife cleaning up and I'm the dog poop in the corner. She's a money vacuum cleaner. You can afford it, it's nothing to you now. I couldn't have known that your luck had run out. Quick, while she's in the bathroom!"

There's no explaining why I gave it to him, and I didn't even intend to tot up what he owed me because I knew I would never get it back.

"You're a sport," he gushed, pocketing the notes with lightning speed. "You're a sport and the Goddess of Luck will reward you."

"Repayment?"

"Next week, next week. I have a scheme."

We all had a scheme, and the pity of it was that none of us knew what the scheme was. It was there somewhere in the back of our minds, but it was perpetually obscure to us.

When Yo Yo returned, we went out to the canal and rode for a while in a gondola under a honeyed moon. It was just like Venice, as it is intended to be, with the water slapping the stones and the moon above gilding insignias and crenellations and gothic devices. Adrian said nothing and Yo Yo and I talked in Chinese, and as we spoke I knew that it was Adrian's luck that had failed to deliver the natural and not mine. I had no idea why I was so sure of this. Eventually we went our separate ways and after a snack at the Florian I walked off back to the Lisboa, and as I was passing through the main doors I caught sight of Adrian sitting at one of the baccarat tables with Yo Yo behind him, his face distorted and blushing, losing with the alacrity and lack of style with which he always lost. So there it was. One loses and one wins, and one submits to the law of sports and pastimes, but I, on this occasion, was off the hook.

SEVENTEEN

The following morning a letter was delivered to my room by the Lisboa management, carried there by a bellhop in full regalia. Unusually for me I was up early, taking my Earl Grey and toast in the room where I was reading the *South China Post*. The mood of happiness from the night before was still upon me, and I felt a kind of self-assurance that was quiet and intimate. It was, if you like, a quiet self-confidence, a sense of being a little bit superior to my circumstances. People with inferiority complexes often feel this way after a few hours of unexpected good luck. The note, meanwhile, was from one of the senior managers of the hotel and invited me to stop by his office later in the day to discuss the unusual scale of my winnings the night before, on which I was congratulated in the politest terms. *It is*, he wrote, *normal procedure when a customer of ours has won such a sum. My ass*, I thought. They always singled me out.

I told the messenger to say that I would be down

within an hour. But as it turned out I was stopped by an elegant young Chinese executive as I made my way to the elevators. He asked me to step into a private office on the floor above. It was, in fact, the writer of the note, a Mr. Chang Souza, and he was as full of charm and precision as an executive can be, in his official Lisboa tie and his cuff links shaped like black dice and his black oxfords with tooled caps. We went into an office opened with a magnetic key and paneled with red wood. There was a juniper bonsai on the desk and a photograph of a small girl in a sailor suit, and Mr. Souza placed himself behind it with a comfortable ease and assurance that seemed intended to make his task easier. On his computer he brought up the transactions in which I had been involved two nights before, and there was a look of surprised consternation on his face as he neared the summit of my considerable tally. "Nine naturals in a row," he said, breaking into a frigid smile. "Never been seen before."

"Not by me, anyway."

"Lord Doyle, you are a lucky man."

"Luck?"

It made him smile. He scanned down my winnings and I was sure that he was skimming through some surveillance videos at the same time. Every moment of every game is filmed; they can be recalled on the company computers in a second. Millions of such moments were captured daily and stored for future use, and they formed an encyclopedia of our gaming experiences. Souza's face was still young, untarnished by pleasure. His eyes, enlarged behind wire-frame spectacles, seemed as if they were blue when they were nothing of the sort.

"As far as we can see," he began, "there is nothing illegal about your winnings. We have been puzzling over it for some hours. I wonder if you are aware of the statistical odds of scoring nine nines in a row?"

While we drank a pot of oolong tea, he asked me if I had played at other casinos around the world before coming to Macau. Monte Carlo, Las Vegas, the Genting Highlands? Or Caracas, the dreadful places in Pailin?

"I expect," he said, "you are a globetrotter, a high roller on several continents, a sharp on the loose."

"Not at all," I objected.

But he laughed; he liked the idea. A lord on the loose. A rogue of the baccarat tables, winging his way around the globe on Bruno Magli slippers. What could be more fine?

For the deskbound managers who actually ran the casinos, such a figure was bound to be irresistibly mysterious. One saw such figures painted on all the walls of the casinos, proud and erect on their Arabian horses, and so when one saw the real thing it was a pleasant surprise. Mr. Souza was one of these sedate managers. For him the world divided into the humdrum—factories, offices, work, labor, sweat salt mines, and mortgages—and the magical sphere of privileges.

He was quite bright with curiosity at this point. His eyes sharpened like needles that will prick their way under skin.

"I've never been anywhere," I said, "except the casinos of Pailin. They were not to my taste."

"No indeed. Khmer Rouge, eh?"

"I was once in Las Vegas. I lost everything."

"They are crooks in Las Vegas, too, I have heard. Terrible, terrible people. But I imagine," he said tentatively, "that you played privately at Oxford, or some such?"

"Yes, privately. Poker."

He sat back and held his teacup between two slender fingers.

"I've always imagined Oxford gentlemen playing poker. Before I was posted here I was running a casino in Jordan for Steve Wynn. A casino frequented by Palestinians."

"Palestinians?"

"Yes. They shot it up in the end."

"Did they?"

"It was against their religion."

"Ah."

"It was a hard experience for me and my family. We were happy to come back to China. Here, as you know, everything is more reasonable. You can pay for anything and get it. Everything is for sale on some level. Do you know what I mean?"

"It's a real talent."

"I think so—sometimes. They call us the Jews of the East. Except that there are one point four billion of us. Imagine one point four billion Jews."

I threw up a hand, and he sensed that he had said enough.

He poured my tea.

"Miss Silva ran a background check on you. She found nothing at all. It is quite puzzling. It's as if you stepped one day out of nowhere, out of a different dimension, and into our little town and brought nothing with you. They tell me there is a code of secrecy among you gamblers, and perhaps you want to keep it that way."

Souza then put down his cup and adjusted his glasses. I had not, as he had hoped, offered any background information about myself, and he had to proceed anyway. I said that he understood my position. Being a foreigner in a strange land, even so denatured and cosmopolitan a place as Macau. He comprehended it to the fullest degree. There was nowhere to turn. One had to be secretive, and he understood it.

He twirled his pen in his hand and looked at me frankly. What did I think I would do with my winnings? I could leave Macau for the mainland and live a lot better for less. I could fly off to Bangkok and live well for a while. The East was my oyster.

"I may stay here," I said.

"I'll come to the point. Some of our Chinese executives are very superstitious. One of them was watching your surveillance videos last night and she swore she saw a figure standing behind you. She swore she saw it, and many of our colleagues believe it. They say that your nine nines cannot be a fluke or a piece of luck. Think of us as superstitious if you like. It's the way it is. My bosses are asking me to ask you not to play again at the casino. It is not even that they are afraid of incurring further losses. They are afraid of the spirit world and they say, pardon me, that you have a ghost attached to you."

"I'd like to see that video."

"There's nothing on it. My boss, I should add, is a very superstitious woman. Her name is Helen. She offered me a rather odd proposition. She said you could play one more hand in this casino. I thought it was an original idea. One hand. You can play it any time you want. Night or day. And then, if you win, you have to leave the Lisboa tables for good. If you lose, we'll rethink. It will prove the ghost is no longer there."

I couldn't help laughing.

"You have to be kidding me, Souza."

"No, all too serious. If you are harboring a ghost, we cannot have you in the casinos. That is her position. Morale among our employees would collapse. It is unthinkable."

"Harboring?"

"I don't know what other word to use. We are not saying it is your fault. Something may have happened—you may have attracted some presence that you are not aware of. It has been known to happen."

"You are telling me a ghost story."

He opened his hands and smiled. *You know how we are.*

I sat very still for a while and digested this change in my situation. I listened attentively to the shuddering hum of the air-conditioning unit, the muted clank of cranes and cement mixers and the sibilance of the computer itself, where my image was no doubt frozen by the pause button. Sounds from a parallel world that did not have my interests at heart. He was not going to tell me what he had really seen on that screen, or what his female colleague had seen, and so from now on we were just wasting time. I wanted to be gone, and yet I wanted to know what the casino would do if I actually won that last hand they had permitted me. I asked.

"You keep it, of course. You keep everything."

From his tone it was suggested that he didn't believe this would happen.

"All of it?"

"It's a casino—of course you keep it. We have a reputation to uphold. We aim to create a true experience for the customer, remember. It's like a journey, a voyage.

We've built everything around that concept of an experience. So your own journey will come to a satisfying end, no? We want you to have a beautiful experience."

"You do?"

"Don't look so skeptical."

But I changed the subject.

"Mr. Souza, do you yourself think that I am haunted?"

He steadied himself and blinked, because now he had to tell the truth. He said that was exactly what he thought, though "haunted" was not the word he would have used. Blessed? At the door, he shook my hand, using that curious mixture of Cantonese and English that people here often break into.

"Gum lei take care la."

Darkness and gold, and the sound of water from afar: the ghosts alive and drinking, tortured by their thirst just like me. I drank heavily in my room. Vodka and cranberry, and gin with lemon twists. I didn't notice the days and nights and the interludes in between where nothing happened. The distant clatter of the casinos, that white noise of the Lisboa, had almost passed out of consciousness altogether. There was a hush to the heavily carpeted corridors, where the staff passed on leather soles with their trays balanced on one hand. The smell of passing waffles and dim sum and bok choy cooked in sauce. The smell of eggs and toast and the *clock clock* of knuckles rapping on doors where men lay half unconscious on their beds in their long black socks waiting for change. I had not had the itch for baccarat for some time. Mr. Souza was correct when he pointed out that worried money never wins.

EIGHTEEN

Two nights later I put on my gloves and placed the totality of my winnings in the Adidas bag. I wore a tuxedo with a white carnation and, in a touch of sad panache, a pair of two-tone shoes. Greased down, pomaded, brushed, and polished, I looked like a cartoon as I left the room with a quiet click and heaved my bag into a gold-plated elevator filled with smoking trolls. The mirror made me think of those incomparable words of Joseph Roth commenting upon a picture someone had done of him: *Yeah, that's me all right, nasty, drunk but clever.* I adjusted the buttonhole and listened to the fools dissing me in their dialects, thinking I didn't understand. And so to the Fortuna VIP room, temple of my baccaratic fate.

I was stopped at the doors by two managers who had clearly been told to look out for me. They were all toothpaste-ad smiles and handshakes, smooth as razor wire and metal to the core.

"Lord Doyle, how nice to see you! Is that a bag full of money?"

"It is indeed," I replied, swinging it with dash. "I had a whim," I said. "I've been away from the tables far too long, and it's time I played a hand or two. You know how it is."

"We're glad to hear it, Lord Doyle. One minute, please."

One of them spoke into a walkie-talkie.

"Would you like a private room?" the other one then said, as they let me in, walking on either side of me. "We can arrange it."

"Not necessary. I like a crowd."

But we don't, they implied.

"Very well," they said. "We understand that it adds to the enjoyment of the game."

"I like to show off, I guess. I'm an old-fashioned exhibitionist. Especially when I lose. Imagine that."

"We have many high rollers like that, Lord Doyle."

"Do you? I wouldn't call myself a high roller exactly. I'm more like a low roller. A low rolling stone covered with moss and pigeon shit."

They tried to laugh at a joke they didn't get. I noticed they wore the same cuff links that Mr. Souza wore: black dice.

"Should we count the money? Most of our high-rolling clients insist on it."

"Sure, count it if you feel like it. Mind if I have a cigar?"

They pulled out a huge Havana before I could make a move. It was clipped and lit in a jiffy.

"Thank you very much. I'll sit here while you count."

They went into an adjoining room and returned in ten minutes. A slip of paper was handed to me with the exact sum written on it.

"Satisfactory," I said. "It's the same total I came to myself."

"Naturally it is."

They bowed.

A waitress in a long, slitted cocktail dress appeared, her face heavily made up. She asked me in Chinese if I'd like a complimentary glass of champagne before I sat at the table.

"Very kind of you. I'll drink it here."

I sat on the heavy Louis XV armchair and sank back into its satin upholstery. The minders bowed again and said that when I had selected my table they would bring the chips to it.

"Fine. But I have one question. I know you have a minimum bet of ten thousand here. What if I bet two million? You know that I am permitted only one hand."

"We are aware of that, Lord Doyle."

"Then I need to know if there is a maximum bet."

This seemed not to have occurred to them.

"I am not sure," one of them muttered. "I will call Mr. Souza."

"You do that. I'd like to know."

"May I ask why?"

"It's occurred to me that I might bet the whole lot on one hand."

"Lord Doyle?"

"You heard me. The whole lot on one hand."

"But Lord Doyle, that is quite crazy."

They laughed at once to offset the possibly injurious implications of such a remark.

"Not," the speaker amended, "that I am suggesting you are crazy."

"What if I were crazy? It doesn't matter as long as you permitted the bet."

"That is true. I was not implying that it would be to our advantage if you bet everything. But I must say, it is. Are you prepared to lose everything?"

"That's my business. Let's say I am."

The conversation with Mr. Souza took some time. The waitresses brought me some complimentary chocolates and I thought for a moment of Dao-Ming and her lovely offering at the Intercontinental. It was a full night and the rooms were smoky, loud, and claustrophobically tense. I heard imprecations and curses from inside the pits, and tightly clustered crowds shouting at a lucky hand. My skin grew cold and prickly. My tongue dried out. Insomnia and dehydration again. Yet again I was going to skin them alive, and if it happened that they skinned me it would be even better. Thus is the yin and yang of the punter's pleasures. Skinning and being skinned are the same. You get to be sadist and masochist not just in the same day or night, but in the same moment. There is something lordly about it after all.

I was on my third glass when one of the gentlemen returned. His look was noticeably apprehensive and he cleared his throat behind a clenched fist before telling me that Mr. Souza had approved the bet.

"I hope, however, that I can persuade you not to make it, Lord Doyle. You have won an enormous amount of money at our tables and in my opinion you would do better to leave with it all now."

"Leave? But I'm just getting started."

"Forgive me, but you cannot be serious. There is only so much you can win from a casino. I would say that you must have reached that limit."

"I don't feel the same way at all. I feel like I am just setting out on my streak of luck."

"Lord Doyle?"

"You know how extravagant we lords are."

"I remember Mr. Souza saying something about that."

"We are complete zanies."

He stiffened.

"But Lord Doyle, you stand to lose every last *kwai*, every last dollar. In one bet. Is that rational?"

"What do I care if it's rational? Nothing in life is rational. Life isn't rational. It's animal."

"Oh?"

He looked highly concerned; his tone implied doubt.

"But Lord Doyle, we have to be rational sometimes."

"Do we?"

I knocked back the last of the champagne.

"Is Grandma rational? Is Mr. Souza?"

"I couldn't say. They try to be."

"Is Guan Yin?"

"Please, keep your voice down. We can't mention that name in a loud voice."

"I have decided to be completely superstitious at last, to trust in the winds. I've made up my mind."

"I'm sorry to hear that."

"Maybe you are. But then again you might win it all back. You must be at least slightly tempted by that outcome?"

"We're only human."

An unfortunate phrase, I thought.

I got up, shedding a flurry of ash crumbs around me.

"It wasn't my idea to have one last hand. It was your idea."

We moved in pantomime toward the private rooms

where the safety-pin millionaires were suffering at the hands of the goddess who was not listening to them. My floor manager made signs to the dealers to stop their motions, and we inspected room after room until I had found the table I wanted. There were six players already there, and it was explained to them that I would be placing an astronomical bet on the table. The buzz went out at once and soon the table was full. I sat at one end and my chips were piled up in front of me. The others were high rollers in their own right, hard men from the southern cities, and there was no mawkish voyeurism in the way they eyed up my pile. They were simply calculating what might be raked in if that amount were put in play. At that moment, however, the second manager came quietly into the room and explained that the table was now closed to everyone except me. They got up, therefore, and filed out with a few incendiary words. The door was closed and the managers remained. I asked for another glass of bubbly and a bowl of nuts. The dealers asked me politely if I spoke Chinese, and I said I would prefer to game in Mandarin, if that was all right with them. We settled down and I noticed a subtle change in the air, as if the air-conditioning had been turned up or the filters enhanced. I felt a little giddy with the alcohol. The manager then leaned toward my ears.

"Lord Doyle, there is a gentleman who would like to play against you. His name is Mr. Cheng. He has asked us specifically. Would you accept?"

I turned and saw an ancient high roller in a Savile Row suit coming through the door with a handkerchief pressed for a moment against his mouth and a look of dour hunger in his eye. TB? He was about seventy, immensely wealthy from the looks of him, and he had come in quietly. He bowed to me and we shook hands. Mr. Cheng from Hong Kong, billions in the bank, and billions out of it, too. I said "Welcome" in Mandarin and he sat at the other end of the table, offloading a sack of chips onto the table's surface and then locking his fingers together and flexing them. We exchanged some pleasantries. Mr. Cheng asked me if it was true that I'd stake my entire pile on a single bet.

"I only have one hand to play," I said. "So I thought I might."

"I might consider matching it."

He had a face like rock, and it was disturbing to watch it move as he spoke.

"I would like that," I replied.

"I have heard about you. They say you are lucky."

"Everyone is lucky once."

Mr. Cheng turned rhetorically to the others.

"The man has some wisdom!"

A hand of baccarat is so short, so abrupt, that the preliminaries are sometimes difficult to disengage from. When the bet is enormous, this is even more true. There is a need among both players and house staff to drag it out a little. So we smoked for a few minutes and Mr. Cheng asked me who I knew in Hong Kong. He was curious. Nobody? That seemed unlikely for a man in *my position*.

"I am rather shy and private," I explained. "It doesn't do for someone in my position, as you put it, to throw himself around too much."

Mr. Cheng certainly understood that. Wealth brings its burdens as well as its pleasures. It is double-edged. He nodded and said that this was certainly correct; it was a malicious and gossipy city, like all cities, and one couldn't be too careful.

"I think I have seen you around," he smiled. "You lunch sometimes at the Intercontinental, don't you?"

"Sometimes."

"I have seen you there."

The dealers prepared themselves and Mr. Cheng looked me over long and hard.

"I never forget a face," he added wistfully.

"I like the view at the Intercontinental."

The managers stepped forward discreetly.

"Are you betting the whole amount, Lord Doyle?"

"I am."

Mr. Cheng divided his chips into two piles, an amount that put together would not be far off from mine. He then placed first one, then the other onto the table and announced that he was betting both on the banker. The cards were slicked out through the shoe, mine first (the highest bettor is always dealt first), and then Mr. Cheng placed a hand over his most leftward card. We waited, and I felt a concentration of perspiration materialize between my eyebrows. It hung there like a stud in a button and then, exposed to the air-conditioning, evaporated. The cards were turned and I had drawn a two and a nine. Modulo ten, that made one. The managers raised their eyebrows and then did not lower them as Mr. Cheng turned a hand of eight with a six and a two. The scores were called and the dealer then dealt me a third card, as was my right, and it happened to be an eight, that most fortunate of numbers in the Chinese universe.

This made Mr. Cheng laugh and he took a drag on the cigar lodged stiffly between the fingers of his right hand.

"Natural," the dealer said loudly. "Congratulations, Lord Doyle."

"You got lucky there," Cheng said quietly, and he said it with a graceful good nature that was apparently genuine. "You have my sincere congratulations."

"Thank you. I would play you a second hand, but the management has decided against it."

"So they told me. I cannot quite understand it."

The chips formed piles like models of cities, and they were not raked together. Cheng didn't even look at them. His eyes were moist and chilled, like oysters, and instead he sneered at the floor managers.

"They are chickens. Mr. Hui, you are chickens, are you not?"

The managers bowed stiffly.

"That's how chickens bow. Look at them. Doyle, shall we go for a drink at least?"

The chips I had won were not gathered into a bag for me. The managers explained that I would be given a check downstairs instead; I could collect it whenever I wanted. They were frostily impressed, as people a little down the ladder often are when they see a flash of undeserved success. *Why couldn't it be us?* they think to themselves. *Why shouldn't it be us?* I said that this was considerate of them, and I went out with Mr. Cheng while the managers followed at a slight distance. We sauntered down the curved corridor and Cheng related to me all the times he had won big at this particular casino. A total of three times in eleven years, he admitted with a roll of the eyes and an expression of pained disgust. These people were crooks, pure and simple, exploiting the weaknesses of helpless addicts. The casino was like a hospital catering to heroin addicts. Inexcusable, if you looked at it sensibly. He waved a hand, as if killing something invisible to the naked eye. The displeasure of a billionaire who has lost one ten-thousandth of a percent of his fortune to crooks. He led me to a bar where aged Scotches filled the glass shelves, including one called Brora that my father used to drink and that was no longer made. We sat in leather chairs. Vivaldi, perfumes, the ease of gentlemen. He spoke softly so the staff wouldn't hear, and he said, "You cleaned them out, you really did. Millions in one blow. They'll be up to see you shortly."

But no one came. They left us alone and we drank half a bottle of port. "You have to understand money," Cheng said as soon as he was toasted. "It trickles through your fingers like sand, but you can keep that flow going if you resign yourself to the forces of chance."

He had made his money as a slum landlord. It was a good living and it kept his wife in her baccarat addiction in the style to which she was accustomed. If he didn't screw the miserable hordes lodged in his rat-infested apartment blocks, how would Mrs. Cheng be able to play the baccarat tables every night?

"Perhaps you've seen her around the casinos? They call her Grandma. It's insulting, but she accepts the name. She's been playing the tables longer than anyone here except Old Song. Have you seen Old Song?"

"I don't think I have."

"Been playing every day since 1947. My wife is more noticeable, however. To the point where everyone knows her."

I kept my cool.

"I've seen her around," I said.

"She's a noted character at the Lisboa, the Greek Mythology, and the Landmark. Those are the three that she likes. The stupid woman never knows when to stop. She knows she has my account to tap into—and yes, I let her, I admit it—and so she goes mad every time she gets near the tables. She has no inner brake. She turns into a money-losing tornado. She's a curse."

I think that was the Chinese phrase: inner brake. Patsy (her real name) was a terror unleashed, but it was a quid pro quo between them, like allowing your wife to be an alcoholic. For a moment he pursed his lips.

"That bloody woman is ruining me! Half a million every night. She's bleeding me dry, and it's just because she thinks I have a mistress."

"Well, do you have a mistress?"

"Of course I have a mistress. Do dogs have tails? But she takes advantage. I play myself, of course—but in moderation. I'm not using anyone except my tenants."

He burst into melodious laughter that was, in some way, not melodious at all, and at the same moment, as if synchronized by horrifying correspondences, his skin broke into handsome rucks like a piece of stretched deer hide that has suddenly been relaxed.

"But that has nothing to do with Patsy. Patsy is in a class by herself. She's a true thief. Patsy *loots* me."

He suddenly leaned forward.

"You haven't seen her here tonight, have you?"

"I've been by myself, as a matter of fact."

"So much the better, so much the better. Preparing

for your great coup! Magnificent sang-froid, if I may say. Not that this is surprising given your background. I have seen a few of your types in action and I have always been impressed by your coldness."

I wondered how much his large pigeon-blood ring weighed, or how a man could even wear one. It was not very discreet of him. He drank his port lustily and the ring winked as his hand tilted. The cuffs were beautifully laundered.

"Money," he sighed. "What a wonderful thing. When it starts *flowing* into you. What a wonderful feeling. It's like drinking vat after vat of the best wine in the world and still feeling thirsty. That's the secret, Doyle. To keep feeling thirsty. Once you stop feeling thirsty you no longer want to keep drinking the wine, and then you're a monk, or dead. Which is worse? I'd rather be dead than a monk. My mother always wanted me to be a monk. When I made my first million she went to the temple and prayed for me. But I never found out what she prayed *for.*"

"For your soul, Mr. Cheng."

"What a word! You are probably right, though. But I kept my soul. It's my bloody wife who is losing it for me."

"By the way," he added after we had smoked our cigars in silence, "are you calling it a night? After your coup I suppose you must be. Always quit while you are ahead. But you know that already. That's what Patsy can never remember."

"I am quitting for the night."

"Excellent idea. May I ask if you intend going back to your room?"

"I have no plans."

He grew visibly apprehensive.

"Do you have a club you go to?"

I confessed I didn't, because the Clube Militar wasn't a club. It was now a restaurant.

"Well, I have a very nice club called the Toga Room. One of these nights—I assume you are tired now—you should come by and meet some of my friends."

He handed me a card with the club's details on it.

"The telephone numbers are strictly private and should not be given out to others. When you call, give them the password I've written on the back."

I turned the card over: the word *invidia*.

"Jealousy," I murmured.

"It's a club for men, so you won't find my wife there. And one word of advice, Doyle. If you meet my wife anywhere in the VIP rooms, do not under any circumstances agree to play with or against her. If you play with her she'll steal everything one way or another; if you play against her she'll lose, and it's my money. Can I count on you?"

"Shall we shake on it?"

He laughed uneasily and held out his hand.

"Why not? I like you, Doyle."

His deerskin face tilted back for a moment and the

laugh was dry. The rich never believe it when one compliments them or expresses any affection for them. They know all the things about themselves that we don't. And I suddenly thought: *I made eleven million tonight.*

"Come to the club, Doyle. Have you ever eaten pangolin?"

He leaned forward again and his breath was edged with Dow's.

"It tastes like penguin and it keeps your hard-on hard. It's the one thing I indulge in that my wife approves of. We can have it fried or boiled with plum sauce. You can have it any way you like. You can have it *battered* if you like."

Seven suitcases of cash were sent up to my room in the morning, just as I had requested. I didn't have a bank account and everything I earned had to be converted into cash. Instinctively, however, the Chinese sympathized with this. Like many Asians, they feel more comfortable with cash than with abstractions. The notes were bundled into units of five thousand and packed into genuine leather cases with handsome locks. When Mr. Souza had left, after expressing his congratulations, I emptied them onto the bed and counted the packets carefully before putting them back into the cases exactly as they had been.

I now had eleven suitcases of hard cash stored in my room, and I no longer thought of leaving them with the management for safekeeping. The balance of power and trust between us had changed and I now thought that they were spying on me, keeping tabs on my winnings and—why not?—my movements. A casino never gives up its money willingly. But they were in a quandary. If they encouraged me to leave now, they stood no chance of ever recovering their losses. Under normal circumstances it would be in their interests to keep me there and to keep me playing. The theory would be that in the long term the odds would be stacked inexorably against me. But they had lost their nerve. They didn't know what to do. If I stayed, I was also likely to be a big spender in the food outlets and elsewhere. I would at least be profitable for them in some way. And so a note came from Souza later that day: *Please feel free to accept our offer of an upgrade to a suite on one of the higher floors.* I accepted and the suitcases, along with my belongings, were transferred to a suite six floors above me. There was a kind of silence around me, and I no longer played music when I was by myself. It was enough to be alone with myself without interference, to sink like a stone into a mineshaft. I went through the casinos after midnight in my new suits as I had always done, and as I did so I felt the weight of the hotel's security surveillance system pressing upon me from all sides. It was, of course, the ban that was in effect against me, and the hapless floor managers in every room had to make sure that I didn't so much as sit at a table. They followed me around with an obsequiously firm hand, and whenever I stopped to watch the play they hovered around me without saying a word.

You can't open the windows at the Lisboa, perhaps because they are afraid of suicides, with so many desperate bankrupts checked in every night—so I slept with the fan and the heating on, with the curtains drawn like a death chamber. Then when I had recovered a little from my strange and slowly aggravating feeling of illness, I went to war again. I took a bath and ate a light breakfast from room service, eggs and toast and tea. It was a little before six and I ordered a bottle of champagne to go with the eggs. I downed half the bottle, then dressed for the fray, though it would not be in the Lisboa. I felt a cold, stable hatred toward the world and toward myself as I went down the carpet-padded corridor with one of my cases filled with about five hundred thousand.

NINETEEN

I was calm as I sat at one of the tables at the Landmark, which here have yellow surfaces and Pharaonic heads. The theme is ancient Egypt and the bar outside the casino is shaped like a full-sized Middle Kingdom ship. The early-morning gamblers sat grimly and thirstily around the table's yellow oval, where their fates were being decided without lifting their eyes. They were unusually rapt, perhaps because they were not the all-nighters but those who had risen bright and early for the game. They were the kind of players with which I was usually unfamiliar. The real fanatics, the guys who get up in the morning to play. The high-stakes table at which I sat had been witnessing some turbulent scenes just prior to my arrival and I had watched the whole thing with interest. Three men in sharkskin suits, smoking heavily, were playing to a small crowd who were goading them on with cries of desperate encouragement. The pallet turned the cards and there was a crushed silence as the banker swept up every single chip on the table. The sharkskins moved away with wounded pride, and for a moment the mood was ugly.

A massive seated figure copied from the Valley of the Kings and an overblown face of Tutankhamen did not mitigate it. I sat down quietly with the chips I had exchanged for the totality of the five hundred thousand I had brought with me and placed a fifth of it—a hundred thousand—on the yellow surface. No one paid me much attention even with such a large bet, and it must have been because the sharkskins had lost much more.

The table filled again. I felt no apprehension at all as I, the highest-betting player, turned my cards before everyone else. The inevitable nine. I raked in as much as I'd laid down and started again. The players sighed and there was a dreary scene. An old lady cried, "Now look here!" and stared at me. Same result. I scooped up my chips and moved to a different table, and the crowd followed me.

I put down a hundred twenty thousand this time and won again. The bankers shot each other unsubtle looks and I played two hands of fifty thousand each. Stiff hands that in normal times would have to be played fearlessly. But I had neither fear nor the lack of fear. I was strung out in between. The first fifty-thousand-dollar hand was matched by the others, who were wealthier than they looked. No one could believe that a player would turn three naturals in a row.

It was like those famous streaks of red that are known

at roulette tables. The ball falls on red for eleven times in a row and the punters, confronted with a twelfth spin, must decide whether there is a statistical law that favors a twelfth red or a black. But ah, there is no such thing as a statistical law when it comes to chance. A pair of dice can fall as two sixes ten times in a row and no law has been broken. If they rolled as sixes a hundred times in a row we'd be astonished—dismayed, even—but no law will have been turned upside down. There is nothing that says the roulette ball cannot fall on red seventeen times in a row (as it does sometimes) or fifty-two times.

I believe a wheel at the Monte Carlo casino in 1897 rolled eighteen reds in a row and a German gambler made a small fortune on the eighteenth because nobody else around him dared bet on red. That man held his nerve. I had now played fourteen naturals in a row, and like that streak of reds my streak of nines was simply coasting along in its aberrant groove. It was one of those things, and the trick was to not succumb to any surprise. I didn't. I played the hand as if it were the first I had ever played. I turned the cards and asked the banker to bag the chips I had won. There was nothing to it, and the spectators went silent in recognition of its inevitability.

Instead of playing the whole amount I'd taken out with me, I cashed in the chips I'd won and placed the united amount in my suitcase. I went upstairs to the lobby of the Landmark hotel and had a pot of tea, opening the case for a moment to look at the rows of banknotes wrapped in rubber bands. It was now about eight o'clock and I was still feeling feverish. Indeed, these attacks of fever were beginning to increase in frequency. I wondered if the Paiza was open at such an early hour. I walked there without any haste and was told that the pits were open twenty-four hours. Therefore, if I wanted to make some bets I could certainly do so, and for any amount I wanted. There was no question of their not remembering me from the previous time. I was shown to one of their private rooms and served another breakfast. I made four bets and an hour later I had won a few million more. The cash filled four cases and I walked out with them as casually as a wealthy housewife walking out of Bloomingdale's with her shopping.

A car was waiting for me at the doors and they wished me a hasty return with at least some show of genuine hospitality. I went back to the Lisboa and stashed the cases next to the others.

It was now obvious to me that my sport and pastime was going through cyclical patterns that were deeper than the usual ups and downs that a player must expect to endure. Bouts of indulgence and triumph were followed by periods of satiation, self-disgust, a determination to desist that had nothing to do with the feelings one experiences during losses. These latter periods of abeyance were getting longer, so that I didn't at all mind cruising from day to day without any visit to the tables at all, and while I lay in my pompous Lisboa bed surrounded by scarlet and gold I read the financial papers with an eye to investing the millions of *kwai* I had earned.

Investing, however, is a big word. I had never had any ideas about that before. I had fully expected to go to seed, and decline in the way that men going to seed decline, day by day, a slow declension marked by ever-diminishing wealth. Winning over and over had seemed like a realistic prospect, and when I won or lost before I had savored both in different ways. Now, of course, everything had changed. The winnings had piled up and they were rapidly approaching the point at which they would render the whole exercise pointless, if the point of it was to win money. Moreover, my health was clearly going into a decline that I could not explain. Fevers, chills, insatiable hunger, none of which had any obvious cause. I reasoned to myself that these were purely psychological, but even if they were psychological, that did not make them any less real. I was sure that I was entering a mental breakdown of some kind, but no two mental breakdowns are ever the same. To the person suffering one, the breakdown always seems slightly unreal. It feels inexplicable.

I speculated on what I could do now if I decided to give up the baccarat lifestyle (for that is what it is) and devote myself to deep-sea fishing, Ming antiques, or Chinese-style ballroom dancing, not to mention real estate and travel. I wondered if I could haul the entire stash of cash across the border using a paid smuggling service, the existence of which was taken as certain in gaming circles. Could I get to Shenzen or even Kunming and disappear all over again, this time loaded with a considerable fortune? Could I stage my own disappearance with enough subtlety that it would ensure that I was left alone to start a new life? But where would I go?

There was Dao-Ming, of course. It had begun to occur to me that I was happiest with her on her island and that I could go back to it and to her. It would not matter if we did nothing for the rest of our lives, just lived in that small house and ate clams every night and made do. It would not be bad; it would be better than anything else. It was possible that I would become like her, a ghost with a place to haunt.

But I knew that it would not happen. I had to turn to other ideas. I thought, in all seriousness, of buying a hotel in Sichuan and becoming one of those absent owners who rake in the profits from a mini golf course while living in a villa by the coast staffed with teenage girls. But it would never happen. And then there was the idea of moving on to another Asian fleshpot. These are the places where Western men come to die. They are our fleshy death-pots.

But first there was the here and now. One morning there was a commotion outside my door and when I went out to investigate I was immediately surrounded by a crowd of local journalists, one of whom had a camera and a boom. They had obviously been waiting there all night, perhaps with their ears pressed to my door.

"Lord Doyle!" they cried, scrambling to their feet and following me down the corridor toward the elevators.

"Lord Doyle," a young woman cried in particular. Attractive, Chinese, bangs, high heels, notepad.

"I am not Lord Doyle."

"Oh, Lord Doyle, can we—"

They blocked the elevators and the cameras rolled.

Lord Doyle, an English gentleman of means, yesterday won seventeen million Hong Kong dollars at the Macau casinos. Gamblers from all over the city clamored to meet him. What is his secret? How does he play? Is he calm or passionate? He speaks Chinese!

"How old are you, Lord Doyle? Can you do math?"

I held a hand up to block the lens.

"You're potty," I said. "I'm not Lord Doyle. There is no Lord Doyle."

"Lord Doyle, are you a Sagittarius?"

"Who told you I was a Sagittarius?"

"So you *are* Lord Doyle!"

"Don't be ridiculous. I am Mr. Doyle."

They all laughed uproariously.

"Lord Doyle, are you a lucky man? Do you pray? Do you eat chicken? Is your mother a Protestant?"

"You can't film me!"

And indeed that was a dangerous thing.

"Are you superstitious? Tell us about the number nine. Do you organize your life around the number nine?"

We crammed into the elevator and I had not even intended to use the elevator. I was being carried along by the momentum and I wanted to escape. So down we went, with the camera rolling and the journalists jammering. I gave up telling them that I was not a lord. They wanted a lord and I was the lord. Word had gotten around so insistently that I was the lord that in the end I simply had to be the lord. As the lord I had to behave in a certain way, and it was a great deal more hassle to *not* behave in that way. So I saw now (as we came down into the lobby and a small crowd of curious onlookers pressed forward to get a glimpse of me) that sooner or later I would just get on with being the lord and that would be easier. The onlookers were gamers who had gotten the word, and since every big winner is a fifteen-minute celebrity in Casinoworld they had to see what the fuss was all about. They pressed around me and asked for autographs or tips or words of encouragement and advice and soon I was brought to a standstill as they formed a closed circle around the news crew.

"Lord Doyle," the reporter continued to press, "are

you planning to play tonight at one of the casinos? We've heard that you've been banned from playing at the Lisboa. Is that true?"

"No comment."

"Lord Doyle, how does it feel to be an English millionaire in a Chinese city?"

"I am glad there are still English millionaires."

I said it in Chinese, and the whole room laughed.

"Are you planning to leave Macau?"

"I'm a private citizen, and I am just as surprised by my good fortune as you are."

"Lord Doyle," a voice asked from the back of the crowd, "is it true the casinos are robbing us?"

"How would I know?"

"Because," the reporter interjected, "your success seems to suggest it."

A few voices rose up: "Yes! They're robbing us!"

The crowd bubbled with an incoherent ill will toward the bosses who took all their money, and the epicenter of this ill will was a goodwill toward me. They practically cheered me as I pushed out onto the street, and the crew followed me with the foam boom hovering above my head. "Look," I heard a voice cry behind us, "Lord Doyle is headed toward the Fortuna!" This was incorrect, and in fact as soon as I was in the street I hailed a cab and went to Coloane for lunch at Fernando's on the windswept little beach across from the Hyatt. There I stayed all day eating asado and drinking gin and tonics and when dusk fell I staggered across the beach, through the tangled volleyball nets, to the imposing hotel, where I got myself a room for the night and spent half of it watching the English Premier League. I was sure that sooner or later my face would appear on TV as well, on one of the local channels, and as soon as it did it would be well nigh certain that Interpol would take an interest. At that moment, ironically, I would have to run.

The intricate cycles of the monsoons, which I have never understood, blew a storm across the bay that night and the cedars and pines shuddered under a veiled moon. I lay in bed burning hundred-dollar notes with a cigarette lighter to see if it would make me feel ill. The hotel was empty, funereal, and I walked through empty halls and empty restaurants where the usual Japanese and Hong Kongers were absent. Paranoia is often like this, and in an empty place we are sure that we are being watched. The waiters, the despondent staff, the idle cooks, they all follow one with their eyes. I sat in the bar upstairs, the one with a sea-view balcony, and I tried to construct a plan for myself. The reality was that the more money I made, the more trapped I felt. Should I play on and on until doomsday, until I started losing again and balance was restored? This is how a hardened gambler would think. It doesn't matter to him, because what matters is the roller coaster, the wind in his hair, the thrill. He plays until he runs out of money.

When I got back to the Lisboa in the morning there was a bouquet of flowers for me in the room and a note from the management. They hoped I would stay on even if I could not play the tables. They had some nerve, but as it happened I had nowhere else to go and my suite was as good as I would get. They apologized for the intrusion from the press. From then on, they assured me, security would deal with it.

Why not, then? The suite was now full of money; bales of it, cases of it, dressers crammed with it. I kept some in the bathroom, some in the cupboards, and the big bills in the digital safe. I stored two cases in the overhead compartments of the armoire and another in the TV cabinet. The air smelled of it, that soft stale scent of human hand sweat and ATM rollers. Cash, the blood of life.

Eventually, having calmed myself with a vat of Kahlúa, my mind turned back to the prospect of the tables and I felt the subtle tug of my pleasure exerting itself once again. I was aware, of course, that the executives thought they were obeying mathematical laws when they permitted me to play on, whereas in fact they were succumbing to a classic case of gambler's fallacy—that is, the fallacy that if deviations from expected behavior are observed in the short term, they must be balanced out by a different outcome in the long term.

This involves an assertion of negative correlation between trials of the random process. Take the example of
tossing coins. The outcomes of each toss of a coin are sta-
tistically independent and the chances of getting heads,
for example, on each toss is always ½. The probability of
getting two heads in two tosses is ¼, and so on. If a player
tossed five heads in a row, the probability of which is only
$\frac{1}{32}$, the other player might assume, according to the fallacy, that a tails is "due" pretty soon. This is incorrect. The
probability of flipping twenty-one heads in a row is, in fact,
1 in 2,097,152, but the probability of flipping a head *having
already flipped twenty times* is, surprise surprise, still only
½. That's what the Chinese don't understand, and now the
bosses were thinking the same way. It was crass and under-
standable at the same time, because deep down they were
sure that something unusual was on their doorstep, that the
spirit world was speaking to them. They were thinking like
locals, which is what human beings always do. They had
simply put aside things that they knew perfectly well, that
every rational person who studies gambling knows back to
front. They knew that this was the theorem of Christiaan
Huygens, well known to every amateur math geek and
card sharp and casino operator worth his salt. Just as they
knew that if two players start out with different amounts
of money—say five cents and eight cents—the guy with
five cents will always, in the long run, lose everything, all
things being equal. But this they had *not* forgotten.

I was now fully aware that whichever casino I went into, I would be watched with maximum attentiveness. But at the same time I knew that they could not believe in my luck continuing because it struck them as irrational— whereas, as I have explained, it was neither rational nor irrational. Accordingly, once powdered and dried the following night—a Thursday, if I remember correctly—I assembled three hundred thousand in envelopes and prepared for battle. The boys from the front desk brought me up a white carnation for the buttonhole, wrapped not in foil but in sheet silver. It was a nice touch, but they needn't have bothered, because in the end something more extraordinary happened.

TWENTY

Since I could wait no longer, feeling starved of my dirty baccarat, I decided to go to the Greek Mythology that evening and throw myself off a dirty little cliff and die. I didn't give a damn, I was *mou bian bei*, as we say in the language, and I wanted if anything to commit baccarat suicide and flame out to the amazement and great concern of all present. What a death!

I went to the Militar and ate some steamed clams. Then I read the papers in the bar, hoping to run into one of my friends. However, no one was there. The evening had the rhythm of an ancient pendulum clock. So much the better, I thought. One is better off alone in these dangerous moments. One is better off forlorn and isolated inside one's gravest compulsion.

I took a cab to Taipa and entered the casino through its overbearing gates. The pits were relatively calm on a Thursday night and I was able to play at a full table without commotion or distractions. I played at table six as fast as I could. Nine all the way, regular as something machinelike. A hundred thousand in fifteen minutes and without breaking even a bead of sweat. *All right,* I thought, *let's attack the system outright.* I laid everything down on five bets and won them all. The chip bags looked like Viking loot, but I did not walk out with them. I kept them by my side and played another three hands, with the same results. At length, the table cleared out and a lanky Chinese man in a windowpane shirt came up to me and whispered in my ear to ask if I'd like some cocaine. It was a done deal and I spent the rest of the hour in the night-club snorting it off the back of a menu, indifferent to the effects. It was good stuff and, as usual, it made me incredibly sleepy. I never get high. I become sleepy, but I get curiously excited at the same time, as if my pulse has been slowed down while my senses have been speeded up. In this state I rolled through the various floors of the Greek Mythology unnoticed by the press and feeling as if I would like to piss all this money out of all ten fingers simultaneously. I slipped five-hundred-Hong-Kong-dollar notes into the hands of the staff, the shills who wait by the tables to lure new customers in—usually attractive young girls—or the Greeks lumbering around in their plastic armor. The look of amazement on their faces was not something that I thought I would ever see again, so I went around again and handed out thousand-dollar notes, and they still didn't know what to say. They took the money and crammed it into their pockets until they had no more room for the next round, and it went on like this for a while, with no one knowing how to stop it. I gave away half of my earnings, then went back to the tables.

The rooms seemed underwater, the smoke static like fish milk suspended in water that isn't moving. I remembered them from that fateful night. Instinctively, but not knowing quite why, I looked for the table where I had met Dao-Ming. The room was mobbed but I found it easily. It was table number four. As I sat there quietly, unrecognized by the staff, I played a winning hand and thought back to that night, which now seemed like a part of my distant past. I had forgotten how long ago it was. Weeks, months, it was all the same. A girl sitting quietly by a table minding her own business, and now I was playing, so to speak, with her money. Needless to say I had not sent her back the money I had taken, and the more time went by the less likely it was that I would ever do it. I was like that, but I couldn't help it. I was like the scorpion in Aesop's fable who stings the animal carrying him across a river. Sorry, I could say (like him), it's just my nature. I won a hand, scooped up the usual winnings, and then just sat there lost in thought with a glass of naughty lemonade. A man in a white velvet suit was playing opposite me, losing mightily, his face red with rage. His bloodshot eyes filled with tender sadness. Where was Dao-Ming at that very minute? I was sad not to know. Was she in a room plastered with mirrors with her legs wide open and her eyes clenched shut? Was she at home making miso soup on the gas ring?

I got up and walked through the wall of smoke. I could see all the flickering numbers at once now. People losing their life savings with a smoldering fag end in one hand, a plastic cup of punch in the other. Old people who must have lived through the Cultural Revolution and its shrill stupidities, who must have known all about point-less gestures. There they were and they should have known better. They were all losing minute by minute, and around them the electronic boards showed the warp of their bad luck. I wanted to shower them with gold to make them stop. They didn't know what they were doing. Thirty years of miserable slog and labor tossed down the maw of the casino in seven minutes. It was incredible. I went to a second table, number nine in the room, and won again, inconspicuously, picking up a nice windfall that I used to clean out a third table. I went on and on until I was at the back of the casino and the Greeks were walking about with vodka shots on trays, their crests of horsehair shining under the lamps. Here there were a lot of these old mainlander couples with their blue caps and their nylon jackets. They played with watery eyes, their veins popping out. The true proletariat from the workers' paradise being milked dry by the capitalists of the new age. They knew it and they enjoyed it, because even being milked dry by the capital-ists of the new age was more novel, more amusing than not being milked dry by them. It was freedom, and freedom is supposed to fuck you over.

The last table was number eight in the room (I was keeping track for some reason), and when I had won there I collected my chips and wandered into the next room along. The light from the chandeliers went straight into my brain and I quivered. Then I remembered the number that Dao-Ming had written on my palm and that, despite a few baths, had not washed off. It was still there, as if written in an ink that could bind permanently to human skin. As I read the numbers I began to realize that in some way they corresponded to the numbers of the tables I had been playing at. It did not, of course, seem possible, but I was increasingly sure that it was the case. A sequence of numbers that must be an irregular phone number could not at the same time be a *plan of action* at the tables, but I thought it all the same, even if I am not one to deny that it might well have been all in my mind, because everything was all in my mind during that time, and I knew it. And since everything was in my mind, everything was equally probable and therefore both possible and credible. I didn't care if the idea was absurd in the extreme, that for me did not make it untrue. It was a sequence, and I was moving through it.

I stood stock-still in the middle of the floor, and I felt overwhelmed with hunger and confusion. *A telephone,* I thought, *I need to get to a telephone.* I went directly out into the vestibule and found one. I called the number in a quiet spot.

I dialed the number on my hand, and I was surprised, hearing the dial tone, that it was a phone number after all. I had nothing prepared to say to her, however. I looked up and saw the clock on the wall, with the two hands aligned on the three. My hands were wet with perspiration and I had to wipe the receiver. At last the dial tone was interrupted and I opened my mouth to speak, to launch into an apology. But no one answered. Instead there was a low susurration at the other end, like white noise, a sound of waves breaking on shingle or flowing in and out of caves. Thinking that it might be a message on voice mail, I waited for three or four minutes, but it continued. The sounds of the sea, continuous and strangely bitter, suggesting the presence of an eternal storm.

I hung up and then, as I was walking back to the tables, I wavered. On a whim, I turned and went back to the telephone and called the number a second time. This time, equally unexpectedly, a voice answered, an irritable old woman.

"Is Dao-Ming there?" I asked in Cantonese.

But they can always tell that you are a *gwai lo*.

"She's out having dinner."

"When will she be back?"

"Who is this?"

"It's Lord Doyle."

"Do you want to make an appointment?"

It had never occurred to me that I could meet her so easily this way. But of course—

"Why yes, I would. When can I come?"

"Let me look."

The phone was put down and now I could hear Hong Kong pop droning from a radio set.

When she came back she was curt.

"I have a spot free at six p.m. next Thursday. Can you make that?"

"Yes."

"Don't be late."

"I'll be there."

"I'm writing you in the book. One hour?"

"Two."

"Ah, much better." She was suddenly polite. "Thank you, sir, we'll see you then. It's ninety-two Queen's Road East near Pacific Place. Take care *la*."

I was so elated that I could only stammer something incoherent. I went back to the tables halfheartedly but then felt enormously hungry and decided instead to dine. I went to Lei Garden and ate urchins and drank rice wine.

As I sat there in that crazy décor with my bag of unused cash I felt bottomless in some way, as if all the urchins I was eating could not fill me. Indeed, I ordered plate after plate and it seemed to make no difference. I was still hungry and ordered more.

As I gorged, I thought of Dao-Ming working from a small room in a tenement on Queen's, cool and business-like, laboriously grooming her hair every day, sealing a little cash in an envelope on Friday afternoons and send-ing it back to her village. She must have paused in front of the mirror and looked hard, perhaps puzzled by what stared back at her, since we have no way of predicting what we will actually become. Time takes us over and does what she wants with us. Even inside our own lives we find our-selves discarded. She pulls a hairbrush through her long mane and criticizes the melodrama of her own mascara. She remembers a boyfriend from long ago, one of the few who mattered, or maybe the only one who did—but they rarely pan out. She wonders where he is now. Married to a proper girl, halfway happy. He will never inquire about her, afraid of the disgrace of finding out where and who she is now. It's better not to know.

She listens to the romantic songs on her radio, waiting for clients. She has not become cynical in the slightest, she is even-keeled and realistic, and her sadness is also even-keeled and realistic. She has passed the halfway point, the point at which realism outruns hope. Her savings are mod-est but rational. She walks all the way to Jardine's Bazaar to eat in the street and she eats alone, among the lovers and the families and the back-slapping businessmen, self-contained and absolutely quiet. She is defeated, but she is not divorced from her pride. She oversalts her food, covers it with hot pepper, and wipes away the tears with paper napkins. She walks through Wan Chai at night with her doggie bag from the restaurant, pausing by the windows of the furniture stores and the pet shops with their cages of brilliantly colored birds. It is not impossible that one day she will own a room that looks like the one re-created in the display, rich with misapplied gold leaf, and that she will fill it with birdcages. One day her luck might turn, as the casinos have taught her.

Night by night, however, her expectation diminishes. She is not waiting for me, or for anyone else. She has given up the extravagant hope that someone might do something impartial for her—or that she might just go home.

So I ate. Scallops made no dent in me, nor did orange duck. For that matter, I was starving for the next two days even though I ate nonstop, night and day. I continued going out, too, yet strangely no one at the Venetian recognized me any longer. It was as if they were watching me from the wings and no one dared interrupt me, or even tap me on the shoulder, but at the same time none of them came up to me and asked if I would like a glass of naughty lemonade, as they had done so assiduously before.

I raked in huge winnings night after night, always playing at the same table at the Venetian, I think it was table number four, and after a week there at table number five, just next to it. I took to wearing sunglasses during those nights, those quiet nights, and my dandy kid gloves that nevertheless gave me the air of a fussy bank teller afraid of getting germs on his fingers. I played cocooned in this way and unaffected by the body odor and the bad breath and the sudden gusts of cold air and the sound of the jongleurs and minstrels weaving their way through the crowds. I played and after I had won I went to McSorley's Ale House, Morton's of Chicago, Madeira and Portofino and Fogo Samba and Lei Garden and Imperial House Dim Sum and gorged myself on steaks, bamboo-pressed noodles, Hakka salted chicken, *mui choy kau yuk* (vegetables with pork belly), *noh mi ap* (rice-stuffed duck), or linguine with clams. Even seated at the table, and only an hour after eating a whole plate of *ngiong* tofu or *kiu nyuk* (sliced pork with mustard greens), I would feel my stomach growl and I would look forward to racing to one of the Venetian restaurants and ordering a meal for three.

I was waiting for Thursday to come, and on that very day, before taking the ferry over to Hong Kong for my appointment with Dao-Ming, I called a cab to take me to the Paiza. As far as I was aware, it was the easiest high-roller place in which to place a high bet, and I had made up my mind to give all my money to Dao-Ming, as I should have done long before. So why not triple it all and make of it a stupendous gift?

When I arrived, the staff recognized me, but with some difficulty, and from their embarrassed smiles I could see that they were perturbed by the drastic change in my appearance that my bouts of fever and hunger had brought about. They bowed nevertheless and one of them took me to the private elevators, even alleviating me of my awkward-looking Adidas bag. We talked about the weather. Inside, the bag was whisked away and I was told the chips would be brought to one of the private rooms.

I asked if these were numbered.

"Not strictly," the girl said.

"If you count counterclockwise," I said, "could you number them up to ten?"

"Of course."

"Then—I am sure you'll understand—I would like to be in the ninth one."

She smiled.

"Don't worry, sir. Players ask for that one all the time, as you can imagine."

"Yes, I can imagine!"

"One minute. Can I seat you here and have you served a cocktail while I see if the room has a place?"

I nodded and sat. I felt quite warm in there, and when the dry martini came I dried my face with the paper napkin. I could see the enormous lantern suspended solemnly in the semidark, the replicas of the Xin terra-cotta army and paintings recessed into the walls. Everything was familiar and yet everything was also subtly altered since the last time I had been there. I felt smaller, shabbier, even though in reality I was in far better shape than I had been, at least from the perspective of the casino. I drank the martini in three even gulps. After fifteen minutes the girl returned.

"There is a place in that room, sir. There are two other players. Would you like to know who they are?"

"It's nothing to me."

"Very well, sir. Follow me. There's no maximum bet here."

"I am glad to hear it."

"Your chips will be here shortly."

It was one of the rooms upholstered in red leather, similar to the ones I had seen and played in before. The walls were papered with pale green fleur-de-lis. There was a tall vertical painting of two English noblemen posed with hunting rifles next to a brace of slaughtered pheasants. As in other paintings, their eyes were very slightly Asian and they looked down at the players with an uncanny precision. A ruined abbey peeped up from behind the painted

willows of a nonexistent England, and beneath this painting a real log fire gently flickered between iron dogs, pok-
ers and hearth brushes slung from a polished brass tree. A
basket of wood lay there as well, lending a faint perfume
to the whole room. Along the mantelpiece stood sponges
and insects encased in glass balls. At either end were two
blocks of books simply painted onto the walls as a trompe
l'oeil, the collected works of Dickens. I came in and saw
my chips assembled neatly at the far end of the table. The
two Chinese players there looked up quickly and shifted
their eyes to accommodate a foreigner who looked like he
had TB. They nodded. They were well-heeled, obviously,
dressed in the city way, in navy blue and gold ties, with
voluminous stockpiles of chips at their elbows. A bottle of
Haut-Brion stood opened on a castered service, with the
cork laid ceremoniously on a saucer. It looked like some
kind of wine-stained insect lying there on a white doily.
I felt warm and bothered as I sat.

We were all introduced and they shook my hand.
Mellifluous English of the British variety, school-induced.

"We were waiting for you," one of them smiled. "Can
we offer you a glass of claret?"

"Why not?"

I took off my claustrophobic jacket.

The wine was served, we raised our glasses and sipped.
Haut-Brion '81: a fine hospitable touch.

The dealer let us find our own moment to get started,

and then asked me very quietly how much I was thinking of laying down for my first bet.

"Well," I said, equally quietly, "I am making only one bet tonight."

There was a small stir.

"One, sir?"

"Yes, I had a dream last night that I could make only one bet tonight. I am superstitious about my dreams."

Everyone nodded.

"I see," the dealer said. "And how much were you thinking of placing on your bet?"

"All of it."

They looked down at the mountain of chips.

I was not sure how this would go down, but the two players were obviously delighted. They broke into jaded grins. I had, apparently, spiced up a dull evening. The dealer noted this and didn't bother asking them formally if this was to their taste.

"Very well," he said. "All of it on one play. Gentle-men?"

We put down our wine and settled in. I was aware—in the next few moments—only of the slight displacements of the burning logs as they shifted and hissed in the hearth, and the heat eating into my right calf. There was a clarity and concentration that I had not felt in some time, an opening of the senses that the approach of danger had provoked. I wore my customary gloves and accepted the traditional privilege of drawing the first card. The dealers moved to the others with a tactful deliberation, a slowness that was mesmerizing to me, and the room was suddenly extraordinarily quiet apart from the fire, like a chamber suspended hundreds of feet underwater. From some distant place I picked up the soft ticking of a wall clock. The second cards were dealt and we turned them simultaneously. I had scored a five. One of the Chinese had an eight. I had lost everything.

I sat back as the chips were taken from me and the great cobwebs of thoughts that had hung inside me for days began to tear apart and fall down. I stopped sweating; I became, on the contrary, completely dry and stationary and composed as I watched my money evaporate into another man's maw. He was congratulated by all present, including myself. The staff were clearly a little sorry for me, or embarrassed at the consequences of my recklessness, and they waited for me to react, to move. When I did, they quietly asked me if I wanted to play again, but so quietly that it was inferred that it would be better if I didn't. Luck was not with me.

As I went out into the vestibule I soaked up the soothing quietness, which was however immediately broken by a loud cheer emanating from one of the other pits. I felt a stab of jealousy, and I was sure that I caught the shrill alto of Grandma's exultant war cry. Perhaps she had won the same amount that I had just lost. I walked on, asking the staff to dispose of the Adidas bag that was handed rather sorrowfully back to me. No matter. I went silently down to the gaming floors and then up again to the Sands casino buffet, where I ordered a rum and Coke and a roast beef sandwich. The floor show that night was a circus from Harbin.

At first there was no conscious thought that my gambling life had come to an end. I looked down at the slot machines at the daily height of their frenzy, the roulette wheels spinning like the cogs of a huge horizontal machine. On the stage, the acrobats in white bodysuits somersaulted through the holes of a tall contraption built to resemble an executioner's scaffold. A large feline, white, was dragged across the stage by a chain. I ate two steaks from Asia's longest buffet, drinking iced tea with them, and then felt the sounds of the casino receding inside me, the movements on the stage turning into blurs. I got up and went down to the main floor holding my head in my hands and threaded a way out between the Klondike and Lucky Slot machines. I wanted to get out of that clean, fetid, nauseating, pop-nothingness air and gulp in the taste of the sea sweeping in on crazy winds. I got to the doors and the staff bowed and I thought I could see, moving ardently toward me through the chaos of the hoi polloi, the head of a manager of some kind whose face was overwritten with the concerns of etiquette and the need for repeat customers. I turned and made off. A Rolls was parked outside the doors and a fabulous woman was roll-ing out of it like a wet noodle. The face was a mask of hard sugar. I didn't want to know who it was. I walked away, out of the glare and into the late-afternoon pallor of the roads, across which the wind swept, waking me up again.

TWENTY-ONE

I took the ferry over to Hong Kong, the boat nearly empty. I felt deliriously happy, though I now had very little to give to Dao-Ming, and I was sure that she would understand. I felt anxious that I would now see her in her real element, without pretense, and that she knew that I was already familiar with this degraded milieu.

I had looked through the call girl websites like 141 that list their offerings by neighborhood, each girl offering a series of demure photographs and providing her cell number and address. There was a time when, driven by loneliness, I used to take the ferry over in the late afternoon and walk to Kimberley Road, where the Venus Sauna entertained many gamblers, and make my way toward Nathan Road until I came to a large and run-down complex called Champagne Court. The upper stories of this place were a warren of hundreds of single rooms of 141 girls, each door covered with stickers in Chinese with prices and recommendations, and sometimes blurred photos of the girls inside. When the girls were busy they hung a sign out-side that said *Please Wait,* or *Well Worth Waiting For.* In here could be found women of offhand, sarcastic beauty, their rooms bathed in pink light and equipped with large mirrors. The men went from floor to floor, most of them young, wandering in the labyrinths where entire subcor-ridors were colonized by courtesans who decorated their ceilings with fairy lights and surveillance cameras. They waited in line to ring the bells that made musical sounds and to see the face peering from around the door. They stated their prices in Mandarin, these mainland girls in gartered stockings.

I had looked for hours on 141 until I found a Dao-Ming in Wan Chai. Most of the girls' photos are heav-ily Photoshopped, and hers was no different. The skin smoothed out, the curves accentuated, the eyes made big-ger. So that it might have been her and it might not. There was no phone number.

I took a cab to Pacific Place, had a drink at the top-floor bar of the Upper House to calm my nerves, and then walked down Queen's Road on the right side until I found number 92. There was a brightly polished metal grille door, as is usual, but no buzzer for the apartments inside. It was right by a crowded bus stop. I had no cell phone so I had to wait until an old man came out with his dog, leav-ing the door open for a second and enabling me to slip

inside. A steep flight of steps led up to the garden courtyard of the usual dismal squalor.

Around the courtyard were narrow apartments with
folding grille gates, some of them open. The old ladies
there cultivated scores of potted plants and diseased cats,
and the cats and the plants lay together in the torpor of
six p.m. as the light dimmed. I went from door to door trying to guess which one was the 141 girl called Dao-Ming.
There was nothing on the first floor, so I climbed to the
second. The grille of the corner apartment here was folded
back and there was a red heart stuck on the door with the
number 141, which is the usual sign that the punter has
found his target. The door was plywood, with a peephole
and a plastic garland nailed to it. Before ringing I listened
for a while, my ear pressed close to the wood, and I heard
a radio playing inside, Chinese pop music exactly like the
kind I had heard during the phone call, and next to it the
sound of a hair dryer. I pressed my hand against the door.
The thought that it might be her was too enormous to
control. And it was also too banal, too outrageous. I rang
the bell.

The radio was turned off at once, followed by the hair
dryer. Silence. I heard a woman in slippers come padding
toward the door. I stepped back and smoothed down my
hair, with the involuntary vanity that overcomes the john
without his knowing it. The peephole darkened.

The eye was there. I hoped she could see me clearly in the fading light of the landing, in the graying light. But if she did, she didn't open the door. She was thinking it over. Sometimes they will not open when they see a *gwai lo*. Our reputation precedes us. I stood there for some time and then I stepped forward again and pressed the bell. It seemed to make a god-awful noise that reverberated through the whole landing. The door snapped open and an ancient, skeptical face appeared.

"Yes?"

"I am here for my appointment."

"Your what?"

"My appointment. I am Lord Doyle."

"Lor' Doyle? Who the hell is that?"

"I called on Friday," I stammered. "To see Dao-Ming."

"Dao-Ming?" she muttered, and her eyes widened.

Her hand held the door firm and she was not going to open it wider. The apartment partially revealed behind her was not a boudoir, could not have been the room of Dao-Ming. It was the disheveled room of an old lady, dour and half-lit and sourly scented.

"There's no Dao-Ming here," she said. "The girl who was here is gone. I suppose I shouldn't tell you."

"Tell me what?"

"So you are one of her clients?"

"Yes—I mean, I was."

"She hanged herself a few weeks ago. All her things were shipped back to China."

I took a step back.

"It can't be," I stammered. "There must be a mistake—"

"No, I cleared up the room myself. There's nothing left of hers here now."

"And Dao-Ming—"

"Cremated at a temple in Kowloon. There was no one to pay the costs."

"Her family—"

"How do I know? Girls like that come and go. They don't have families."

I tried to think of something to say, to prolong this conversation in the face of her growing irritation. And the door was closing—

"Not even one member of her family," I cried.

"No one knew where she was from. Probably too poor to come to Hong Kong. Maybe they shipped her ashes—"

One of the other curtains had now parted and a prying face had appeared. What was the *gwai lo* doing on their landing talking in such heated tones? The old lady shrugged and the door began to close.

"But where can I find out?" I whispered.

"What's there to find out? It's over. Go home and find another whore."

With this final flourish of annoyance, the door slammed shut.

I had to leave. I began to descend. At the first floor a few families were out on the landing eating at folding tables. I went past their knowing stares. The next flight of steps was narrower and more malodorous, and at the bottom of it the streetlights glared through the metal gate. I was halfway down them when I heard a door opening on the second floor and I stopped again. From far above, falling through cracks and chinks in the stairwell, a shaft of light fell downward until it struck the steps around me. I looked up. Surely someone had come through a door and was going to come down the steps. I went softly down to the gate and put my finger on the buzzer that would open it. Suddenly the street looked garishly anonymous, women standing full-lit in front of a huge furniture store next door, mentally mapping out their future kitchens and dining rooms, and around them commuters with pinched expressions hustling their way down Queen's Road. The usual crush of a Hong Kong evening. I then turned and looked back up the steps and I could sense the person coming down the flight above it, but carefully, without sound, perhaps taking it step by step. I pushed the buzzer. A wave of terror rolled over me as the metal gate swung open and the perfume of passing women washed over me. I looked back for a moment before stepping into the street, and I saw someone turn the corner, a woman's pumps and bare legs, a quickening pace. I went into the street and let the gate snap shut behind me. As I strode away I heard the buzzer ring a second time.

I now walked uphill on Queen's back toward Pacific Place. I could have glanced behind me but I didn't; I walked on as fast as I could, in a straight line, knifing through the wall of bodies, anxious to escape into the comfort of the great corporate space at the top of the hill. I decided not to take the elevators inside the mall and instead slogged up the steep path that runs around the side of the development. As I rose up this hill I looked back once at the traffic intersection by the small underpass where the pedestrians were massing by a red light. From out of the underpass a girl was walking, quite distinct among them, her long hair brushed forward over her face. She stopped with the others and there was something chillingly apart about her, about the way she stopped and looked up at me as I turned and trotted up the hill, sweating and panting and struggling with my own unfitness. When I got to the top I didn't look back again. I rushed into the plaza where the Shangri-La and the Marriott stand and made for the Upper House again. I went straight up to the bar of the Café Grey, with its views over Victoria Harbor.

When I was truly alive—once upon a time—I loved

this bar. It was my favorite bar in Hong Kong, and for some strange reason I have always felt safe here, anonymous, able to drink without interference. I love looking across the warehouses in Tsim Tsa Shui and the neon that says, or rather asks, *What's your number?* Other of these mysterious signs spell the words *Prudential* or *Still Growing.* I look at the empty lots of construction sites lit by arc lamps. Cranes standing by the water's edge, as if about to explode into meaning. The dark wood furniture, the pretty girls, the cocktails that would cost a welder a week's wage. This was where I liked to get tanked. A wealthy man here can just fall into a suite designed by Andre Fu if he's too drunk to walk.

I sat and got a cocktail with a ridiculous name and downed it in a minute. A wild fear still had hold of me, and I watched the new arrivals coming into the Café Grey from the corridor by the elevators. The girl with the mad hair did not appear, but what was to stop her from waiting for me downstairs in the lobby? I was sure for a while that I was being hunted. But it might have been the booze. I suddenly felt immensely alone. The room began to shrink. I gripped my banknotes, the last few I had hidden away, and they tumbled, somehow, onto the bar like confetti. The barman asked me if I was all right, but I hardly heard him. The girls were looking at me as if I had leprosy, as if I were about to die on the spot. I could see what they were thinking. An aging gambler on the rocks, capsizing minute by minute. A man with fear in his eyes, teetering on the edge of self-control. But then again it was maybe because I had lost so much weight and was by now little more than a skeleton. Either way, it was clear that they were anxious to get rid of me, that I did not fit in with their elegant and youthful atmosphere. At length a manager came up and said that I was looking a little ill. Would it not be better if I went home?

"But I want another drink. You're a bar, aren't you?"

"Yes, sir. But we have to look after our customers."

"So I can't order a White Russian?"

"I think it would be better if you didn't, and went home instead. Really, sir. You are dropping money all over the place." His eyes glanced over my shoulder to make sure that there was no kind of scene developing around us. "I cannot expose my staff in this kind of situation. And it would not be fair to you either. Can I call you a taxi downstairs?"

"No need, young man."

"Do you live in Hong Kong?"

"No, Outer Siberia. But I can walk home."

He motioned to one of his waiters.

"Can you take the gentleman downstairs and make sure he is all right? Call him a taxi and charge it to the house."

I slid off my stool and staggered to the elevators, shadowed by the nervous waiter. We went down in an awkward gloom. As we came out into the plaza he asked me about the taxi and I declined.

"Where are you headed?" he asked.

"I'm going to clear my head and walk around. Don't worry about me."

I went back down to Queen's Road and walked along it for some time in the direction of Jardine's Bazaar. It was still rush hour and the crowds had not thinned out. The parks were open and I wandered into one, the shadows massing across it, and lay down on one of the benches. The trees here, banyans or figs, I could not tell, closed out the sky and I was able to doze even in the thick of the noise and bustle, and soon in any case the streets died down and a quiet returned. I slept then and some hours must have passed.

Homeless people are discouraged in Hong Kong's neat and prosperous parks, but no one came to rouse me and send me on my way. The night became mellow and easygoing, and I slept into the early hours, dreaming in my way of all the things that I didn't dare to think about. The moon rose between the gleaming and implacable towers, and in the park I opened my eyes and thought of the tropical forest that this island must once have been. An island of fig trees like these, magnificent with fruit and monstrous roots. And as I woke slowly, almost unwillingly, I was aware of a hand placed upon my forehead and someone sitting next to me, quietly waiting for me to rejoin the world. It was like that moment at the Intercontinental, which now seemed so long ago, when I had understood finally that the supernatural is real after all. The hand was like a poultice, damp and cold but reassuring, and the form contained neatly in its elegant silk clothes was almost maternal. We said nothing, and indeed, looked at from the point of view of eternity, there was nothing to say anyway.

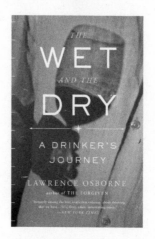